Trapped

Samantha Alexander lives in Lincolnshire with a variety of animals and a schedule almost as busy and exciting as her plots! She writes numerous columns for newspapers and magazines, is a teen-age agony aunt for Radio Leeds and in her spare time she regularly competes in show-jumping, dressage and eventing.

Other books in the

Hollywell Stables series

1 *Flying Start*

2 *The Gamble*

3 *Revenge*

4 *Fame*

5 *The Mission*

HOLLYWELL
STABLES

Trapped
6

Samantha Alexander

MACMILLAN
CHILDREN'S BOOKS

First published 1995 by Macmillan Children's Books

a division of Macmillan Publishers Limited
Cavaye Place London SW10 9PG
and Basingstoke

Associated companies throughout the world

ISBN 0 330 34200 2

1 3 5 7 9 8 6 4 2

A CIP catalogue record for this book is available from
the British Library

Phototypeset by Intype, London
Printed by Cox & Wyman Ltd, Reading, Berkshire

Chapter One

"You've got to help me!" A spiky-haired girl wearing Doc Martens and a cut-off T-shirt sat in our kitchen looking washed out and desperate. She said her name was Hazel. "You're our only chance," she sobbed. "I don't know where else to turn."

Sarah, our stepmother, passed her a tissue and Ross, Katie and I didn't know what to say for the best.

"He's just a baby," Hazel said, "he's only four years old."

Hazel had turned up on the doorstep at eleven o'clock that night, deeply distraught and hardly making any sense. We had taken her in, listened to her story and tried to get her to calm down. In the beginning all she kept saying was that we had to save him. Then she had started to open up and the full details came out; it was even more bizarre than anything we could have imagined.

My brother Ross asked what we'd all been wondering: "Surely a horse that young couldn't be crippled with arthritis?"

"He had an accident – about a year ago – twisted his fetlock. It never healed properly. He was put back into work too soon, it's all that woman's fault!" Hazel broke down in a fresh bout of tears and Sarah suggested she stay the night as she'd missed the last bus home.

"Arnie's the only thing I care about," she said. "Without him there's no point carrying on."

Arnie, it turned out, was a seventeen hand German bred Hanoverian and the best horse in the world. He was steel grey, as strong as an ox and liked a pint of Guinness a day. We still had no idea who he belonged to or where he was being kept.

"You've got to tell us more, Hazel, we can't help you unless you help us!" Sarah knelt down in front of her, wiping her eyes with a tissue. "Who is Arnie? Who does he belong to?"

It was our job to save horses. This is what we were here for: to listen to people's stories, help, come to the rescue. We'd done it time and again, but it never got any easier. The idea of this beautiful young horse facing a death sentence made my blood boil.

Hazel pulled a creased photograph from her pocket and handed it to Sarah. "Here, this should tell you all you need to know."

It was a tatty picture about the size of a school photograph but it obviously told a thousand stories. The colour drained from Sarah's face.

Ross took one look and passed the picture to me. It was a portrait of a woman dressed up in top hat and tails holding on to the head of a huge grey horse. The woman was Jennifer Beaumont, affectionately known as Bo in horsey circles. She was a famous dressage rider. She was blonde, thirty-something, and extremely well liked. She was smiling, oozing star quality and looked totally above reproach. The horse was nuzzling against her hair. It was the perfect photograph.

"That's Arnie," Hazel said in a strangled voice. "That's my baby."

"I don't believe it," I said, stroking Oscar who was purring half asleep on my knee. "I always thought she was so nice."

Hazel had gone off with Sarah to get some aspirin. The poor girl was heart-broken and I couldn't blame her. Apparently she'd looked after Arnie since he was first born. He was always a

3

big-boned thing, clumsy and gawky and they'd given him the show name Goliath. Hazel called him Arnie, after Arnold Schwarzenegger, the film star, because he didn't know his own strength. He was as gentle as a lamb but always getting into trouble. He was easygoing, somewhat lazy and totally unco-ordinated. But amazingly when he was in the dressage arena and forced to work he could perform beautifully. He was so powerful even Jennifer Beaumont found him difficult to sit on. He was a rising star and destined for the top, that is, until the accident.

"It's so tragic," I said, looking at the photograph again and the horse whose career had been so cruelly cut short.

"But he doesn't deserve to be put down." Ross collapsed into an armchair, raking a hand through his jet black hair. It was well after midnight but we hardly seemed to notice.

"It's all about money." Sarah came back into the kitchen with Hazel. "Apparently the lovely Ms Beaumont is in debt, she's having to sell horses left, right and centre. Arnie is insured for a lot of money. Now he's classified unfit to work she can have him put down and claim the full insurance payment for loss of use."

"But that's dreadful," said Ross, struggling to

come to terms with what Sarah had said. "Arnie has literally become salvage."

"But why can't she let someone have him for hacking and just pottering around?" I suggested. "He could have a really good life."

Sarah put some teabags in the pot and turned round to face us with tears glistening in her eyes. "Because he's insured for ten thousand pounds," she said, "and he's worth more to Ms Beaumont if he's not around."

"But what kind of woman is she?" I said, my voice quivering.

"Heartless," Ross answered, folding over the photograph and placing it back on the table. "Completely heartless."

I couldn't have agreed more.

"So are you going to help me or not?" Hazel's eyes stared unblinking at Sarah, defiant, trying to hide the fear of us saying no.

It was seven o'clock in the morning. We had talked well into the small hours as to what we could do to help, how we could save Arnie's life. Hazel had just come inside – she'd been up with the lark and had already mucked out six stables. She was a total professional and left us all standing.

"So?" she said, her elfin face smudged with dust and sweat.

"You didn't have to do the stables," Sarah said.

"I know. I wanted to. So have you made a decision?"

"It won't be easy," Sarah began.

"I know that already," Hazel snapped... "Look, maybe I'd better just go . . ."

Hazel turned for the door, nearly stumbling over Jigsaw, our golden Labrador, who was sprawled out on the stone floor. She reached for the latch and stopped in mid air.

"You'd better write down the address," Sarah said. "We haven't got much time."

Chapter Two

"Somerset Stables, it's just outside Staunton – here, turn left here!" Hazel leant over the front seat giving instructions to Sarah.

We flew over a tiny crossroads and then came to a grinding halt as Hazel tried to get her bearings.

"Mel, pass me that map, I think you're sitting on it."

"It's at the right page," I said, sticking the map under Sarah's nose.

"She's bound to listen to a sanctuary," Hazel's voice tailed off.

I didn't like to tell her I wasn't so sure.

Somerset Stables was every bit as impressive as I imagined: superb immaculate stables, two all-weather arenas surrounded by white fencing, picture-book fields with beautiful mares and foals.

"This must have cost a fortune," Ross said,

who was sitting next to me and gaping through the window like the rest of us. Only Hazel was oblivious to it all, wound up and uncommunicative.

"She's there," Hazel pointed to a woman on a big bay horse. "It's her."

There was no mistaking Jennifer Beaumont. She was the centre of attention.

"Darling that was wonderful." A blond horsey-looking chap sat on a shooting stick, shouting encouragement across the arena.

One of the grooms ran across carrying a mobile phone and the bay horse momentarily shied away.

"He's over here." Hazel moved across to the first stable in the row and a big grey head appeared with soft brown eyes and a floppy bottom lip. "This is Arnie!"

Before we had chance to draw breath, "Bo" Beaumont had ridden across, talking into the mobile phone. "Hold on, sweetie, we seem to have got some kind of school party here." She put her hand over the mouthpiece and looked daggers at Hazel. "How many times have I told you that we simply don't tolerate visitors."

Her voice was acid-sharp, spiteful. She was not at all how she appeared in magazine pictures and on television.

"We're from Hollywell Stables." Sarah's voice was level and reasonable.

"Oh," Bo said. "I see."

Bo had dismounted and was shaking her long blonde hair. "I don't see that it's any of your business."

"Anything to do with horse welfare is our business." Sarah was holding her own.

"The horse is a waste of time," Bo said, getting angry. "He's no good to anybody."

Arnie nodded his head over the stable door, flapping his lips to amuse himself, totally unaware of the significance of the conversation.

"Give me ten thousand pounds and you can have him with pleasure." Bo picked up her reins as if to dismiss us.

"You know we don't have that kind of money," Sarah insisted.

Bo just shrugged and turned her back.

"I'm appealing to your better nature." Sarah was fighting a losing battle.

"Forget it, I've said my piece."

"Come on, darling, go through it once more and then we'll call it a day." The guy on the shooting stick tried to get Bo's attention again – he didn't even acknowledge us.

"You'll regret this," Sarah shouted after her, but she didn't seem to hear.

Hazel threw her arms round Arnie's neck while he gently butted her in the face.

"We won't let you down," I told him, finding a soggy mint in the bottom of my pocket.

"Too right we won't," Sarah said, narrowing her green eyes as she watched Ms Beaumont flounce back into the arena. "We'll re-group and come up with Plan B. And if Miss Fancy Pants wants a war, then that's exactly what she's going to get!"

Trevor, our full-time groom came bounding across the yard as soon as we opened the car doors. "Where have you been? I've been trying to contact you all over the place."

"Trevor, what is it? What's happened?" Sarah asked, worriedly.

With purple hair, Union Jack shorts and builder's boots, Trevor was the most unlikely groom anyone could imagine, but he'd proved himself to be loyal and was now a bonafide member of the Hollywell team.

"You mean you didn't see that bloke in the Jag shoot down the road?" he asked.

"Trevor, you're not making any sense," I complained.

"Oh my God, but he is," Sarah groaned, filled with horror and dropping her car keys on the cobbles. "That was . . ."

"Maxwell Curtis," I said, suddenly putting two and two together.

"Maxi Crowface more like," Trevor scoffed.

Sarah groaned even louder.

Maxwell Curtis was the local MP and extremely wealthy and influential. We'd been trying to arrange a meeting with him for weeks with the idea of him putting a bill forward in Parliament to stop the live export of horses for meat, but it was like talking to a brick wall. He'd finally agreed to a meeting but with all the excitement over Arnie we'd completely forgotten. Now we'd proved unreliable and he'd had a run-in with Trevor. I was convinced he'd never take us seriously again.

"Well it's no good crying over spilt milk," Sarah bounced back. "I'd better go and give him a ring."

"Oh and some geezer left this." Trevor held out a business card. It was for an insurance firm and someone named Derek Hatfield. "He said he'd call again."

We didn't give it another thought.

"Coeee!" Mrs Mac, our official secretary shouted from the office.

"She's going round the bend," Trevor grunted, about to make a quick getaway. "I think she's had too much sun."

Poor Mrs Mac did look mildly hysterical, but then not without good reason.

"I don't think any of you realize the gravity of the situation." She was waving a wad of papers up and down as a make-shift fan while she reached for a lemon bon-bon. "We've been let down in a big way."

"I see what you mean." Ross checked the figures.

"But I thought we were doing so well," I said. This was the last thing we needed – a major crisis.

Ever since we had come back from France with a lorry-load of rescued ponies we had been organizing a petition to stop the export of live horses abroad to be sold for meat. We had appeared on radio and local television. We had appealed to every riding school in the country. The weekly paper had collected ten thousand signatures; Trevor had single-handedly collected a thousand traipsing round pubs and bowling alleys; I had spent every Saturday in the High Street with a clipboard and pen – everybody at school had put down their name.

But according to Mrs Mac it wasn't enough. We had set a target of one million signatures and we were three hundred thousand short. What's more, the presentation was at Number Ten Downing Street in just under a week's time.

"What are we going to do?" Mrs Mac started to panic.

"I wonder if we'll have a police escort?" Katie carried on regardless. "We might even be invited in for afternoon tea."

"Get real, Katie," Trevor barked. "You'll be lucky to see a secretary, never mind the PM."

Katie insisted her "stars" for that day predicted something out of the ordinary, but I was more concerned about the horses escaping into the streets of London. We were taking Queenie, our lucky mascot who was partially deaf and brilliantly behaved on special occasions, and Colorado, who was now a famous show-jumper and used to lots of noise and flashing cameras. Katie said she was going to wear her Hollywell Stables T-shirt, and I planned to buy some new jodphurs and jodphur boots. Heaven knows what Trevor was going to turn up in – his purple hair was bad enough, but we couldn't possibly exclude him.

"This is serious." Ross sat back on a box of Hollywell mugs.

"We'll just have to get out there and make up the shortfall," said Trevor, optimistic as ever.

"The whole reputation of Hollywell Stables is at stake," Ross said. It was the truth.

"I know." Mrs Mac sounded at the end of her tether. "You don't have to remind me."

A few hours later, Roddy Fitzgerald raced up the Hollywell drive in his clapped-out Mini, tape recorder, paper and pen at the ready. Roddy was a reporter on the *Weekly Herald* and a really good friend. We'd never forget his heroic attempts in dealing with a hunt saboteur called Zac, and although he wasn't very good with the horses, he really liked them. In fact Roddy had been the first person to join our fan club.

"So where's the big white chief?" he grinned, as he unfolded himself from the car and rubbed his knees. "She's promised me an ace story."

This was Plan B. To go to the media with a vengeance. Sarah had been on the phone all morning, and we had already raised quite an interest in Arnie's plight.

"Sounds a real character," Roddy commented.

"Who, Arnie or Hazel?"

"Both."

Jigsaw finally got the message that Roddy didn't really want him jumping all over his nice clean suit, then Katie dragged him off to see some of our new arrivals, in particular Walter, our wayward mule, who promptly snorted all over his starched sleeve.

Mrs Mac said she didn't recognize him with his trousers on (last time she'd seen him, Roddy had been stripped to his boxer shorts – but that's another story).

"I'm ready for action now." Roddy pointed to the tape recorder, and I had to admit he did look more professional.

Sarah came out of the house, deep in thought, clutching on to six dripping ice-cream cornets and nibbling at one of the flakes.

"There's been a development," she announced. "And it could be in our favour."

We all held our breath in a state of expectancy.

"It's Hazel – she's been given the sack!"

Chapter Three

"It's unfair dismissal." Hazel had arrived at Hollywell in a desperate state and nothing we could say would calm her down.

"I'm not leaving Arnie with that witch, I'm *not*. I don't care if they have to drag me bodily out of his stable."

As soon as we had left the yard, Bo had gone berserk at Hazel and given her two days to pack up her things and go.

Sarah was straight on to the Industrial Tribunal, and Roddy was literally writing the story as we spoke. Hazel gave him the picture of Arnie and one of herself at the National Championships, and Roddy promised a page lead in tomorrow night's paper. Sarah was keeping her fingers crossed that one of the major Sunday papers was going to ring back, and the local television station was at that moment informing their crew of the situation.

"This is what we need," Sarah insisted. "The

last thing Bo Beaumont wants is bad press. It'll kill her perfect image stone dead."

"But it's not enough." Hazel wouldn't be convinced. "It's all going to take too long – we've got to do something now!"

Ross passed her a cup of sweet tea, which she refused, and I tried to reassure Jigsaw, who was wondering what on earth was going on.

"Hazel, you've got to trust us, we know what we're doing." Sarah tried to calm Hazel down.

"But do you?" She took us all by surprise. "You've not been open that long, have you? Can you honestly say you've dealt with this situation before?"

Sarah was as cool as a cucumber. "Go and look at the scores of happy faces out in the fields, I think you'll find your answer."

Hazel burst into floods of tears and ran out of the room.

"Trevor, go after her," Sarah said, after a few minutes of deathly silence. "She's upset, she didn't mean it."

The rest of the day was a lot less frantic. I managed to scrub down two winter rugs and hang them on the washing line to dry, and to take the pressure off Mrs Mac, Katie and I spent some time packing up orders for fan club members. We'd recently started a new line in Hollywell Stables pencil cases and bags and they were selling really well. I couldn't believe the amount of money people would spend, but I certainly wasn't complaining. It was the general public who were the life-blood of the sanctuary. Ross showed some visitors around the stables: a family with four children. The mother was nearly in tears when she saw Sally, our little blind pony, and heard her rescue story.

Trevor had disappeared with Hazel. I was beginning to wonder whether he'd be back for evening feeds. We were all worried and upset for Hazel and Arnie but I had every faith in Sarah – she wouldn't let Arnie be put down. I also knew that if anyone could console Hazel, it was Trevor: he had a heart of gold.

"That was the police on the phone." Ross had answered it in the tack room. "Apparently a donkey has been stolen in the area. It's pure white. They just want us to keep a look out."

Both the police and the RSPCA tended to keep us informed of missing ponies, or of anything that might be of interest to the sanctuary. I always felt a pang of heartache whenever anyone mentioned stolen animals. I could still remember vividly when Bluey had been stolen from our field and the heartbreak we'd all gone through. I wouldn't wish it on anyone.

"Not much chance of us finding it, though," Ross said. "It could be anywhere by now."

Trevor rolled up just as Mrs Mac was putting the final touches to a huge home-made pizza, and I knew something was wrong when he didn't immediately drool at the mouth. He even refused a portion of Mrs Mac's apple crumble which had always been his out-and-out favourite.

"Trevor, if you were a horse I'd be seriously worried."

"But only if I were a horse, eh?"

I didn't have time to give him an answer. Katie shot through the door like a startled whippet, her face as white as a sheet and her mouth gaping open.

"I've seen it!" she finally managed to shriek out, dropping a tub of chocolate ice-cream all over the floor, which Jigsaw thought was wonderful.

"The axe man! I've seen him!"

"Katie, what *are* you talking about?" Mrs Mac demanded. Katie had always had an over-active imagination, but this was ridiculous.

Trevor coughed uncomfortably in the corner

and suddenly became intent on burying his head in the fridge.

"Trevor, have you been filling her head with tall stories?" Mrs Mac was determined to get to the bottom of this.

"It was a ghost! At one end of the upstairs windows. Just staring out. Watching. Waiting to get me."

Katie's dark eyes expanded to the size of two flying saucers, and it was a full ten minutes before we could coax her to say anything else.

"There's no such thing as ghosts." Mrs Mac flung the dishcloth at Trevor which clipped him on the ear.

"Trevor was just winding you up." I tried to reassure her. "He does it sometimes. He thinks it's called a sense of humour." I pulled a face at him for being so irresponsible.

Apparently Trevor had told her that the Old Rectory, an eight-bedroomed, almost derelict house on the edge of the village, was haunted. The axe man had murdered his family and then killed himself, and his ghost roamed the empty rooms unable to come to terms with his guilty conscience.

"You didn't see anything," I insisted. "It was just your imagination."

"Funny though," Mrs Mac meditated, when Katie had left the room. "I could have sworn that old house was boarded up years ago."

"Mel, leave me alone, I'm not telling you," Trevor and I volunteered to do evening feeds and we were bringing in three ponies each from the fields and being dragged all over the place. We didn't bring all the horses in, just the ones who were really old, or needed special treatment. We were all convinced that any day now we'd have terrific thunderstorms. This heat-wave couldn't last for ever: the grass was disappearing away to nothing, and it was so oppressive.

"You'll find out tomorrow," Trevor insisted, not giving anything away. He'd asked Sarah for the morning off and I knew he was up to something but he wouldn't tell me what.

"It's to do with Hazel, isn't it?" I asked, grabbing hold of a hairy Welsh pony who was trying to devour a tub of begonias.

"No," Trevor answered back, a little hastily. "Now mind your own business."

*

It was Katie who first spotted the huge red horse-box trundling up the lane taking up the entire road and brushing against the over-hanging trees.

"It's Blake!" She came tearing across from one of the fields, Jigsaw going crazy under her feet. "He's back!"

My heart leapt in the air and did three triple somersaults. Blake was back.

I dived out of Queenie's stable, nearly colliding with one of the free-range hens and suddenly became painfully aware of my unwashed clammy hair, my bright red face and a spot in the middle of my chin. I looked a mess. No, even worse, I looked awful, and there was no time to get changed – the horsebox was already turning up the drive.

"Don't worry, sis, you don't look any worse than usual," Katie quipped.

I lobbed a dandy brush at Katie and then gave a low groan of despair. Blake was in the driving seat still dressed in his white shirt and show-jumping jacket and wearing dark sunglasses. He looked as if he'd just stepped out of a Hollywood film set. If anything he was more gorgeous than ever.

"Life's just not fair," I whined, trying to cover

over a patch on my left knee. "Why can't I look like Michelle Pfeiffer?"

"You're fine just as you are," Trevor grunted, filling up a water bucket and causing me to go redder than ever – I didn't realize I'd been speaking aloud.

"Move the wheelbarrow!" Ross ran forward as it nearly disappeared under the huge modern cab. "More to the right." He waved his hands like a traffic warden. "Watch the wall!"

The horsebox finally came to a halt with a swish of airbrakes and Blake leapt down, grinning all over his face. He looked different somehow, more confident, more sophisticated – but still the same Blake. He and Ross were very similar, extremely dark, although Blake was a few inches taller and altogether leaner.

"Well don't just stand there," he said. "What about a proper welcome?"

"You look so different," I managed to say when Sarah had finished hugging him to death.

I was still worried that my hair was all over the place and I'd got my chin tucked into my chest in the hope that my spot wasn't glowing like a beacon.

"Come here, you daft thing," Blake leaned across, almost in slow motion, and ruffled the top of my hair and then gave me a massive hug. My face turned scarlet and I could have throttled Katie when she started singing, "Here Comes The Bride." Trevor looked really uncomfortable, and Ross asked wasn't it time we got Colorado out of the box before he kicked a hole in the side?

Colorado was a beautiful 14.2 hand skewbald, half wild Mustang, half thoroughbred, who we'd rescued from a girl called Louella. He was now a grade A show-jumper and one of the best horses in the country.

Blake had just returned from the Royal International Horse Show. He and Colorado had been away since Easter competing on "the circuit" and hadn't been due back for another three days. I knew because I'd been counting them off on a calendar.

Colorado came pounding down the ramp like a champion. He looked even more powerful than ever and twice as spirited.

"He's getting very cocky," Blake joked. "It's all the attention."

I led him into the stable next to his old friend, Queenie, who was neighing at the top of her voice, and Colorado whipped round and very nearly followed me out again. We left them together to catch up on old times while Sarah said we had enough of that to do ourselves, and what did Blake know about Jennifer Beaumont?

"There's no dirt on her, if that's what you mean." Blake sat down at the kitchen table. "At least not that I know of. She's always been so squeaky clean. Unfortunately it's not against the law to have a horse put down because it can no longer do its job."

"We've got four days," Sarah said, revealing that she'd just spoken to Roddy and that Bo had decided to extend the deadline on Arnie's life by an extra two days. "She's just trying to take the heat off herself, make it look as if she's doing all that can be done. Her vet is trying a new form of treatment but according to James if arthritis has set into the joint, there's nothing that can be done."

James was our local vet and Sarah's fiancé. He was brilliant because he could answer any question on anything.

"One thing's for sure," Blake said. "Bo will hate you for any bad publicity, especially at the moment, when she's trying to get a new sponsor."

"I know," Sarah said with a thin smile, "which is exactly why we're going to step up the campaign."

Mrs Mac plied Blake with more food than he'd seen in two months. On the road Blake said most up-and-coming showjumpers ended up living off hamburgers and what they could cook in their horseboxes.

Katie was fascinated with stories about Hickstead and wanted to know if the Derby bank really was as steep as it looked. Blake said he'd never ridden down it but it was even worse than it appeared on television.

Mrs Mac nearly fainted with relief when Blake passed her a box of nearly one hundred thousand signatures. It was a fantastic achievement and totally unexpected. Apparently the petition had been passed around audiences at all the major shows and behind the scenes.

Katie was bowled over when she read some of the names. "Half the Olympic team have signed!" she squealed.

"And there are some eventers, too," Blake added. "There's even Mark Todd."

"So when are we setting off for Downing Street?" Blake grinned.

"As soon as we find another two hundred thousand signatures," Sarah said. "Anyone believe in miracles?"

*

"Trevor fancies you," Ross hissed in my ear as soon as we were alone together by the sink.

"Don't be so stupid," I hissed back, nearly dropping one of Sarah's best plates.

"He's not said a word all night and he keeps glaring at Blake."

"Well I haven't noticed," I lied, feeling the colour welling up in my face.

"No, because you've been too busy drooling over Blake."

"I have not!"

"Sssssh," Ross nearly pushed the tea towel into my mouth. "The question is, what are you going to do about it?"

We returned to the table just as Sarah was giving Blake a rundown on all the latest residents.

"And at least Sally's cataracts don't seem to be getting any worse, and the ponies from France are all doing very well."

"And Mrs White's daughter's getting married next week." Mrs Mac brought out yet another one of her chocolate cakes. "And the Post Office is up for sale."

"So who's moved into the Old Rectory?" Blake asked quite innocently.

We all stared at him with our mouths open.

"A big man," Blake said. "I saw him at one of the upstairs windows as I drove past in the box."

Katie's face drained of colour. "You've seen him, too," she said in a small voice.

"The question is," I joined in, "*who is he?*"

Chapter Four

"Trevor has been arrested," Sarah said as she put the phone down.

It was the following morning and I'd just sat down with a pile of biscuits and a cup of hot coffee. It was half past ten, and Blake had promised me a ride on Colorado. I was just about to change into my jodphurs.

"You're joking," I said. "You've got to be!"

Trevor had left at the crack of dawn and I'd been itching to find out what he was up to, but getting arrested – Trevor?

"Come on," Sarah started frantically shutting windows and locking doors and accidentally stood in the cat litter tray. "We've got to get to Somerset Stables as quickly as possible!"

Blake drove while Sarah filled us in on the story. It had been Bo Beaumont on the phone and she was spitting with fury.

"That woman's got an evil temper," Sarah said,

practically bursting a blood vessel herself as she ransacked her purse for some change.

"Not a bit like you then," Ross grinned as we turned down a lane, which Blake insisted was a short cut.

It was another boiling hot day and I could already feel my T-shirt sticking to my back. A DJ on the car radio said, "Hi groovers, isn't this weather just great?" I said I wished it was snowing, and Katie for once agreed with me.

"You still haven't told us what's going on." Blake crunched the gears and started hanging out of the window as some horses came into sight.

"I think there's your answer," Sarah said in a solemn voice as we rounded the next bend.

Somerset Stables had an impressive entrance with huge iron gates and wonderful lion statues on either side. But it wasn't them that we were staring at. It was the hordes of protesters grouped outside the gates chanting and marching up and down with placards and banners. And in the thick of them was Trevor.

"What on earth does he think he's doing?"

Hazel was leading the show, sitting on the bonnet of a blacksmith's van, refusing to let him through the gates. Two other girls waving a wooden board started shrieking even louder,

"Save Arnie! Murderers! Animals have rights, too!"

The blacksmith looked bewildered. Suddenly I noticed Bo, with two police officers, strutting through the fray with a face that looked as if it was going to crack with rage.

"It's all their fault." She pointed accusingly at Sarah.

One of the police officers with ginger hair, who I vaguely recognized, put his hand on Trevor's shoulder. "You're going to have to move on mate, this is private property."

He wasn't under arrest. Obviously Bo had been exaggerating.

"But this is a peaceful picket," Hazel objected, refusing to get away from the van.

"Come on, duckie, it's time to clear out."

"But you don't understand." Hazel started fighting him off. "This is our only chance."

"Hazel, listen to me, this isn't the way to save Arnie." Sarah had rushed forward and was trying to grab hold of her free arm. "What use are you going to be in a police cell?"

"Well, at least I'll get some decent publicity," she yelled back, tears streaking down her face.

The blacksmith continued to stare and the

police officer rubbed his knuckles where they'd sliced against the wing mirror.

"Breaking the law, is that how you're going to win the public's sympathy? Use your head, Hazel, for God's sake!"

Most of the other picketers had left as soon as they saw the police officers. Trevor was the only one left holding a banner. I noticed that the paint had run on the word "Arnie."

"But it's not fair," said Hazel. "It's just not fair."

"Here, you can take these with you!" Bo Beaumont flung a rucksack, a horse blanket and a pile of clothes on to the gravel. "And if I ever see you on my property again, I'll set the dogs on you, do you hear?"

"But you can't just throw her out," Trevor protested. "She's got nowhere to go!"

One of the grooms who had fetched Hazel's stuff rushed forward and pressed a necklace into her hand. "Don't lose it," she whispered. "It was for your birthday."

We took Hazel back to Hollywell. Sarah said she could use Danny's room as he wouldn't be back for two weeks because he was staying with his mother. Gradually Hazel calmed down, and Roddy confirmed that the story was going in the paper that night. Hazel insisted on making herself useful outside and spent the next couple of hours grooming Jakey, Walter, Dancer and Queenie. I'd never seen anybody bring the body brush down in such regular even strokes. She was amazing. Katie was fascinated when she got a full demonstration on how to plait up, while I sidled off to Colorado's stable, drained and exhausted and in need of five minutes to myself.

I sank down in the deep straw with my eyes closed and Colorado nuzzling at my hair. It was another ten minutes before I realized Blake had come in and was sitting beside me.

"You must be getting old when you can sleep during the day," he joked.

"I've missed you," I blurted out, instantly regretting it.

"Me, too," he said, taking hold of my hand. "And he'll be all right you know, we will save him."

There wasn't much we could do about Arnie but there was something we could do about the petition.

"We can't just leave it all to Mrs Mac," Blake

reasoned. "Besides, it'll help take our minds off Arnie."

We decided to go out collecting signatures, all round the local villages. It wouldn't make a tremendous amount of difference but it was a step in the right direction, and it would please Mrs Mac.

Trevor refused to come with us. What's more, he was downright rude to Blake. It all started when I wanted to put Colorado in the field. Blake asked Trevor to fetch the headcollar. It was an innocent remark and I knew Blake didn't mean anything by it. But Trevor went off the deep end.

"Fetch your own gear," he yelled. "I'm not your servant. Next thing you'll be wanting me to valet your horsebox, or would it be to polish your boots?"

Trevor stormed off in a temper and Blake just gaped in total shock.

"I knew something like this would happen," Ross said, putting an arm round my shoulder. "You've got to sort it out, sis, you can't string them both along."

"But I'm not," I protested. "Trevor's my friend and Blake's my . . ."

"That lad's got an attitude problem," Blake

came back from the tack room carrying the head-collar.

"No," Ross said, opening Colorado's door. "He might be a bit rough around the edges, but Trevor's the most loyal person I've ever met. He'd stick with you through thick and thin, and that counts for a lot."

Ross, Blake and I eventually set off with a clipboard and pen. Katie stayed behind with Hazel who was busy showing her how to make a bat box, of all things. Katie had been watching a wildlife programme on television and was determined to attract more bats to Hollywell. Ross said all she had to do was stand in the orchard after dark and they'd all come flocking.

We had hardly got to the end of the drive before a car turned up and a bald man in a suit wound down the window. He asked if Sarah Foster was on the premises. We told him to knock at the front door. He said his name was Derek Hatfield. Yet again, I didn't give him a second thought.

It was so hot. I was wearing a cropped white T-shirt, denim shorts, which showed off my white legs, and scruffy old trainers. I was still boiling hot.

"Where now?" Ross said after we'd knocked on a dozen doors and had nearly been attacked by three Jack Russells. We still had the old part of the village and three cul-de-sacs to complete. Blake suggested a choc-ice each from the local shop, and I said it was the best idea he'd had all day.

"Talking about ideas," Blake went on, "what about a visit to the Old Rectory?"

I dropped my choc-ice on the pavement, "You *are* joking?" With all the panic over Arnie I'd completely forgotten about the new mystery resident.

"That place gives me the creeps," Ross said, visibly shuddering. "Whoever's moved in must be mad – it's like a morgue."

"I agree with Ross," I said. "Wild horses wouldn't drag me up that drive."

"Well that's settled then," Blake said. "Come on before you lose your nerve."

The drive was circular, very elegant, with a huge poplar tree in the middle of the front lawn, and acres of neglected garden and rose trees running wild. In its day it must have been fantastic but now it was just falling to pieces.

Ross pushed open the iron gate which creaked on its hinges. Everything was so quiet. All I could hear was my heart pounding and my feet crunching on the gravel. I felt like I was taking the yellow brick road in the *Wizard of Oz*, only I was the lion and I'd have given anything to run back home to safety with my tail between my legs.

"I don't think this is such a good idea," my voice rattled, somewhere in my throat.

"Don't be silly." Blake grabbed hold of my hand and we marched forward. "There's no such thing as ghosts."

The front of the house was stone grey with steps up to the main door and most of the lower windows boarded up. Lichen and moss were growing all over the place; it had that damp, clingy feeling that made you think of graveyards.

"Look, over there." Blake pointed to the back of the house. "Somebody's definitely living here."

There were sprinklers turned on, gently rotating over the shrivelled brown grass.

"Doesn't he know there's a hosepipe ban?" Ross took hold of the huge door knocker and rapped it up and down three times. I gripped the clipboard until my knuckles turned white and broke the top off the pen with my other hand.

Nobody answered the door. Ross knocked again. Nothing.

"I think it's a fair assumption to say he's not in," Blake said, swivelling round on his heel and looking over the vast lawns and flower beds.

Ross moved towards the back of the house.

"I don't think we should be doing this," I said, my knees starting to quake. A cloud passed lazily over the sun, and it became more creepy than ever.

Blake and Ross didn't even hear me. They'd found a ladder leaning up to one of the back windows which was wide open. The ground around the base of the ladder was strewn with ivy clippings. A tatty piece of netting was wafting back and forth in the breeze. It was impossible to see inside the ground floor windows.

"Look, let's get out of here before he comes back." My voice was rising to a screech now. "This is stupid!"

Blake put one foot on the bottom rung.

"Maybe she's right." Ross was the first to change his mind. "Whatever's going on in there, it's none of our business. We don't want to be done for breaking and entering."

"Yeah, you're right, but you've got to admit, it's pretty weird," said Blake.

We turned round with every intention of leaving. I was practically falling over myself to get down the drive. Then we heard an eerie sound.

"What was that?" Blake stood stock still with his hand on my arm. I looked up at the open window but there was nothing to see but the flapping netting. Surely it couldn't have been what I thought . . .

"Listen . . ." Blake put a finger to his lips.

Time almost stood still as we strained to hear the slightest noise.

There it was again. No doubt about it. And it was coming from inside the house.

"Oh my God." Ross's face turned white.

Horror slowly filtered through my body.

The donkey kept on braying for a full five minutes.

We were climbing the ladder after three.

"Hurry up," Ross shouted as he clambered through the window. Blake followed him in and then leant over to give me a hand.

We were in a bedroom with an old brass bed which was covered in cobwebs. There was no carpet, just floorboards and the door was ajar. We slipped through not knowing what to expect.

The hallway was huge, dark, murky, with a kind of musty smell which pointed to years of neglect. I put my hand on the banister and felt the dust clog under my fingers.

"Come on Mel, quick!"

Blake and Ross were already tearing down the stairs. I could hear the donkey now as if it was right next to me, I could hear the panic in its voice.

Blake flung open a door. Ross was right behind him. Suddenly there was a loud clatter from a room on the right. Blake swung round and took a step forward.

"No!" I shrieked, wanting to reach out and stop him. I had a crazy notion that the donkey was a ghost and it was leading us to some terrible fate.

"Blake!"

He pushed open the door.

I was bounding down the stairs now, two at a time. All I knew was that Blake and Ross had disappeared and the donkey had stopped braying. It was deathly quiet.

The room looked like an old library, only there were no books on the shelves and all the furniture had been pushed to one side and covered with a big dust sheet. There was a huge bay window looking out over the back gardens and a door on the opposite side of the room leading to heaven knows where.

Blake and Ross were kneeling down in front of the fireplace. That's when I saw the donkey. It was snow white with the cutest face I'd ever seen and it turned and stared at me as if I were its guardian angel. It wasn't a ghost at all – it was a real live donkey, and by the looks of it, not very old. .

"He's gorgeous," I said, burying my hand in his white coat mingled with flecks of grey. He pricked his ears up and tried to push his nose into my pocket. I offered him a mint and he wolfed it down and started pawing at the floor with a foreleg. "Oh, you poor baby, who's done this to you, eh? Who do you belong to?"

Blake gently examined his teeth and said he was probably not much more than a year old. He'd got a full set of deciduous teeth.

Behind an old sofa were two saucepans full of water and there was a wedge of hay lying near the fireplace. Somebody must be looking after him, he obviously hadn't been abandoned. But what was he doing locked in the library of an old deserted house?

"Put two and two together," Ross said. "Remember what the police said, 'A white donkey has been stolen.' I think we've just found him."

I didn't know much about donkeys apart from the fact that a male is called a jack donkey and a female a jenny, but why would somebody steal a donkey and hide it away? How much were they worth?

"We'd better call the police." Ross stood up and moved towards the door. "We've got to get the little guy out of here before he hurts himself."

I didn't see the shadow in the doorway. Neither did Ross. Not until it was too late.

"What the hell do you think you're doing?" The voice was well spoken, but high pitched, out of control.

I wheeled round, panic grinding inside me. We were trapped with nowhere to run.

A six foot bloke in a pin-striped suit loomed in the doorway, glaring at us with white hot anger.

But it was what he was holding which filled me with cold dread . . . a shotgun, and it was pointing straight at us!

Chapter Five

"I've got to do this." The man yanked a piece of baling string tight round Blake's wrists. "You do understand, don't you?"

Understand? Understand that a man with a shotgun was tying us up in a deserted house? What were we supposed to do, sit back and thank him?

Ross kicked my ankle and hissed under his breath. "Cool it, will you, we don't want to get our heads blown off."

Panic was rising inside me. This couldn't be happening! The baling string dug into the soft flesh above my wrists.

"Do as you're told and you won't get hurt." The man propped us up against the settee and stood back to look us over. He was about forty years old with blondish hair. His suit was soiled and ripped around one of the pockets and his shirt was open at the collar with the tie pulled loose. "One wrong move and you're done for, do you hear?" His hands were trembling; he was as panic-stricken as a cornered animal, but he wasn't joking.

I cringed back against the settee hardly daring to move. I was frightened now, petrified, but I couldn't help blurting out, "But you can't leave us here, you can't do this!"

The door slammed shut with a sickening thud. We heard his footsteps on the stairs and then silence. He was gone. Only the donkey carried on munching at some hay as if nothing had happened.

"We've got to get out of here." Ross tugged at the string to get his hands free but it was no good, it was too tight. Our legs were bound, too.

"I think he's locked the door." I started dragging myself forward on my bottom.

"Listen, wait," Blake said. "It's no good wasting energy uselessly. We've got to stay calm. Work out a plan."

"But he could come back any minute and kill us." Tears were stinging at the back of my eyes. "Blake, I'm frightened."

"Well he's definitely a nutter," Ross said. "Did you see how his eyes were all glassy?"

"What are we going to do?" I was nearly

crying. "Everybody's going to wonder where we are."

"Exactly – we just sit tight and wait."

"I don't know whether you've noticed," said Ross, "but we haven't got much choice."

We didn't know whether the man was coming back; we didn't have a clue what all this was about. If Katie were here she'd be convinced he was a drug smuggler or an axe murderer. All we knew for sure was that we couldn't escape. We literally couldn't move.

It was really odd. Somehow the reality of the situation hadn't hit me. It all seemed like a terrible nightmare and any moment now I'd wake up and be back at Hollywell. Only I didn't wake up. The door opened instead.

The man walked in carrying a tray and I could smell baked beans before he'd even got near us. There were three tins of coke on the tray and a bar of chocolate.

He didn't untie us. He took a spoon and hand fed us, one mouthful each, one at a time. I felt like a baby bird in a nest, totally helpless. He wiped some tomato sauce from the corner of my mouth with a napkin. Then he held up a can of coke so I felt the cool liquid drain down my throat.

"I can't let you go," was all he said. His hands were still trembling and veins in his neck stood out like cords. In fact his whole body was set rigid, a time bomb just waiting to go off.

"Why are you doing this?" Ross asked.

But the man didn't answer. He just gave us a look of disgust, picked up the plates and marched out of the room. Once again we were left by ourselves.

"Any ideas?" Blake said eventually, after we'd discussed all the reasons why we were here, talked endlessly about Hollywell and dreamt about Mrs Mac's apple crumble.

It was dark outside. I'd got pins and needles in my arms and Blake said his hands had gone numb.

"I don't know how much more I can stand," I croaked.

"If only we hadn't climbed up that ladder," Ross said.

"But then we wouldn't have found the donkey." I tried to be positive.

"I hate to say this, guys, but I honestly don't know what we're going to do." Blake at least was being honest.

"I wish I'd paid more attention to murder mystery movies," Ross joked.

We had no ideas – we were trapped in a room with a donkey, no food, no water and no hope. All we could do was sit and wait . . . That's when I must have dozed off to sleep . . .

The banging at the front door jolted me awake like an electric shock.

"Somebody's found us!" Ross tried to heave himself up.

The door knocker rapped hard up and down. The man came flying into the room carrying a roll of masking tape.

"Shut it," he growled, tearing off a strip and slapping it across Blake's mouth and then Ross's. I pulled my head away and tried to yell out, "Hel . . . p" but he grabbed hold of my hair, and before I knew it the tape was across my mouth, too.

"Be good," he threatened, straightening his tie. I noticed that he'd had a shave and brushed his hair. I also saw that he had pulled a curtain across the main window so nobody could see in.

The banging at the door continued.

"Hello, can I help you?" I heard his voice at the door. He sounded so normal. "I'm sorry I didn't hear you, I was watching television."

"I wonder if you can help us. We're looking for three teenagers, two boys and a girl with long blond hair. They should have been back hours ago." It was Mrs Mac – her voice was starting to break. "We're desperately worried."

I was silently screaming now, pushing at the tape with pursed lips but it was not making the slightest difference. I now knew what it must be like not to be able to talk.

"I'm sorry, I haven't seen anything. I've been at work all day, only just got in, actually."

Blake tried to reach a coffee table leg with his ankles.

"Have you recently moved in?" This time it was Trevor.

Blake inched his way forward.

"Only been here a few days, I'm renting it off Mr Johnson. Bit of a dump really."

"You've got your work cut out." Trevor was being friendly.

Blake wrapped his ankles round the ornate wooden leg.

"So if you see them you'll let us know?" It was Mrs Mac. "We're from Hollywell Stables, just down the road."

Blake tugged at the leg but nothing moved.

"No sweat, they've probably just lost track of time."

"I dearly hope so," Mrs Mac said. "But it's so unlike them."

Blake pushed with both feet and the coffee table and a huge antique lamp went crashing to the floor.

But it was seconds too late. The front door thudded shut, blocking off any noise or disturbance. Mrs Mac and Trevor might as well have been three thousand miles away. The man came in, took the tape off our mouths and left.

"It's twenty-four hours before the police can do anything." Ross sounded so defeated.

I'd never felt so sore in all my life. The only respite we'd had was when the man took each one of us to the toilet, but always holding on to the gun. There was no escape in the bathroom. The window was boarded up, it was all so hopeless. It was now the middle of the night and we were trying to get some sleep.

The donkey dozed near the fireplace, every now and then snorting and shuffling to keep his balance. He didn't seem at all bothered about us in the corner. I think he realized we didn't have any food for him. He'd been left some carrots and vegetable peelings and he'd munched his way through those.

I shuffled my position to get more comfortable and leant on Blake's shoulder. Outside an owl hooted and I thought I heard a cat on the roof. I shuddered even though I wasn't cold and Blake turned his head and kissed my hair.

"Sweet dreams," he said, half asleep. "And keep thinking it can only get better."

The sunshine streamed in through the window the next morning and the man burst in, full of beans, shouting, "Rise and shine!" as if it were perfectly normal to keep people tied up all night as prisoners.

"I've got a special treat for you this morning," he grinned like a totally different person, reaching for the donkey's saucepans to fill them with fresh water. "You're going to really like it."

He came back with a steaming bowl of lumpy porridge as if it were a special gourmet offering. "Just what you need to keep your strength up," he said. "Susan used to love my porridge."

Who was Susan? And why was he suddenly being so nice?

He held out a spoonful in front of me and I didn't dare refuse. It tasted revolting and I was sure the milk was off but I just moved my jaws up and down and swallowed. The last thing we wanted to do was upset him.

"How long are you going to keep us here?" Blake was trying a new tack. "You're going to get in serious trouble you know, you'll end up in prison."

There was no answer.

"What's the donkey's name?" Blake asked.

"Snowy, his name's Snowy. And I'm Joe. Now cut the questions."

He told us he was going out for a little while and that we were not to try to escape because there was no way out. He left us with a radio which was a link with civilization at last. The DJ whom we had heard yesterday came back on air. "Another fantastic hot day out there, groovers. Perfect for just laying back and doing nothing." It seemed a lifetime since we'd been to see Arnie.

He played a couple of romantic ballads and then some heavy metal from a local band who'd just landed a record contract, and then it was straight to the news at eleven o'clock.

"Three teenagers by the name of Mel and Ross Foster and Blake Kildaire have been reported missing after setting out to collect signatures for a petition to stop cruelty to horses. Blake Kildaire is a bit of a local name, an up-and-coming show-

51

jumper, and Mel and Ross are from the well-known horse sanctuary, Hollywell Stables. If anybody's seen or heard anything, please report it on this number . . ."

He then gave out our home telephone number, and I felt like shouting, "We're here, help, do something!" But a bright, breezy pop record came on next. Nobody could hear us. Not even the birds outside.

"We've got to come up with something," Ross said, trying to shake his hair out of his eyes. I'd got a terrible itch in the middle of my back and a fly was irritating me to death as it kept trying to land on my arm.

"If only we could get Snowy to come across here and undo us," I said, wallowing in wishful thinking. But things like that only happened in books and this was real life. We had to think of something practical.

Slowly as the hours ticked by, and there was still no sign of Joe, we formulated a plan. It wasn't a very elaborate plan but it was the best we could come up with in the circumstances.

What we didn't expect was the unexpected.

Snowy had been dozing in his favourite spot by the fireplace, resting on three legs. The smell from his droppings and staling was now getting pretty bad, but in our situation it seemed the last of our worries. Joe came back into the room with a bundle of hay and started shaking it out on to the floor. I don't know whether it was the way the sunlight slanted, or Joe's hand movements, but Snowy suddenly leapt back, jerking his head up and stepping into the hearth.

His near hind-leg locked tight. I don't know how it happened but it terrified me. The whole length of his leg was paralysed and just hanging stiff as a rod. Fear rolled around in his eyes, his nostrils flaring in panic. He tried fighting against it but nearly lost his balance. Joe had his hands up over his eyes.

"Keep him still," Blake shouted out, instinctively fighting to free his hands. "For God's sake man, hold him still!"

Joe was getting hysterical. "Not again, oh not again, I can't stand it."

Snowy was breathing heavily but his own good sense stopped him from struggling. Ross looked as horrified as me. I'd never seen anything like it!

"Let me go," Blake demanded. "Undo me and I can fix it."

Joe didn't seem to hear him. He just started silently crying to himself and refused to look at Snowy's leg.

"Joe!"

Minutes seemed to drift past. But it was only seconds.

"He's dislocated his patella – he's in pain, Joe. Let me put it back," Blake insisted.

That seemed to do the trick. He fumbled across to Blake and started undoing the knots. "No funny business though, do you hear me?" His fingers clasped firmly around the gun which was lying on the chair. "I mean it!"

"It's happened before hasn't it?" Blake examined Snowy's leg. "There boy, steady, it's going to be OK. The ligaments haven't developed properly. Look, we might need a rope."

Joe held the gun. "It normally just goes back by itself."

"Not this time." Blake was down on his knees. "It's too bad."

"No rope." Joe released the catch on the gun. The tension was unbearable.

"I'll do my best. Now you'd better hold his head."

Snowy was quivering all over. His huge ears had flopped back and he was watching Blake out of the corner of his eye.

"I'm going to count to three and then I'm going

to try and push it in. Hold him tight . . . one, two, three . . ."

The sudden snap made me wince.

"It's in," Blake breathed.

Joe went ecstatic. For vital seconds he completely forgot that we were his captives. He just kept patting and rubbing at Snowy's neck, laughing and crying at the same time.

That's when Blake seized his chance.

He grabbed Joe from behind and lurched for the gun.

"Traitor," Joe screamed out and dug back with his elbow.

"Blake," I yelled.

Joe spun round with superhuman strength. Blake regained his balance and moved forward. I could hardly watch any more. The gun was suspended in the air with them both wrestling for a stronger grip. Blake's foot tangled in a ruck in the carpet and I could see his knee buckling. Joe was pulled down with Blake's weight. It was all a horrible situation, a terrible accident. And it happened so quickly.

"No," Joe yelled . . . and the blast filled the room.

Chapter Six

"Blake!" I stared down at his wan, lifeless face. "Blake!"

The blood slowly seeped through his white shirt.

"You've killed him." I was verging on the hysterical. "You've killed him!"

"Calm down you silly nit-wit, I'm still here." It was Blake. He was talking!

"Get an ambulance," Ross shouted.

"Blake, if you bail out on me now I'll never forgive you." Tears were pouring down my face. "Blake, do you hear me? Don't you dare leave me. Who's going to teach me to show-jump if you're not around and who's going to ride Colorado? Blake, are you listening to me? I . . ."

"I know." He was still alive.

As soon as Joe had untied us, Ross started ripping Blake's shirt open. "It's just a graze, it's caught the top of his arm," he said. "I'm going to make a tourniquet."

Thankfully, Ross had been on a first aid course. It didn't look like just a graze to me. There was blood all over the place.

"Did you hear that, Blake, you're going to be all right."

"Well, I could have told you that," he mumbled.

"In that case there's no need for an ambulance," Joe was standing directly behind us with the gun.

"You've got to be joking." Ross could hardly believe it. "He needs proper medical care, surely you can see that?"

"It was his fault," Joe said. "He shouldn't have been so stupid. Now he's got to pay the price."

I was starting to get really frightened.

Ross rolled up a strip of the shirt and tied it at the top of Blake's arm.

"At least get us some water and antiseptic," I pleaded, silently deciding that when the police did catch him they should throw away the key for ever.

I dabbed at Blake's forehead which had broken out in a sweat and prayed that an ambulance would magically appear, but I knew there was no chance of that happening – Joe had no intention of dialling 999.

"There's some cartridge lodged in his arm." Ross washed the blood off his own hands in one of Snowy's saucepans. "If he doesn't get help he could get an infection, maybe even blood-poisoning."

Joe's face didn't even flicker.

"You monster," I yelled, standing up, my hair all over the place, my whole body grubby with dirt and sweat. I'd had enough now. I was fed up with being bullied by this madman. I wanted to go home. "I hate you," I yelled. "I hate you, I hate you! I hope you rot in hell."

Ross put his arms round me and I started crying, sobbing, all the fear and panic of the last twenty-four hours coming out.

"If you don't sit down and be quiet I'll tie you up again." Joe's voice was jittery, on edge – he was starting to lose control.

"Do as he says, Mel, it's our only chance." I couldn't believe how well Ross was handling all this. Usually it was me who stayed calm and together.

Joe pulled something out of his pocket and handed it to me. It was last night's paper and on the front page was a picture of Arnie, his big goofy face staring out at me. "Does this horse deserve to die?" – Roddy had really gone to town with the headline.

"Tell me about Hollywell Stables." Joe sat back in a chair, nursing the gun.

I didn't have a choice. So I started to talk. He wanted to know every little detail. Every horse we'd rescued. All about Sarah and Mrs Mac and Trevor. I was exhausted.

That's when he started to cry. I was embarrassed at first, I'd never seen a grown man cry before.

"The bleeding's stopped," Ross said, examining Blake's arm. "Keep him talking," he hissed at me.

But it was Joe who took up the conversation.

Susan was his wife and Snowy belonged to her and their two children, Charlotte and Emily. A few days ago she'd walked out on him, taking everything. In a fit of anger he'd stolen Snowy from the garden late at night and brought him here. He knew she'd report it to the police. If she was going to take the kids, then he was going to have Snowy, it was only fair.

It was obvious something must have flipped in his mind – the gun, keeping us tied up here – for the first time I realized he must be a very unstable man.

"At Hollywell we give good homes to animals like Snowy," I said. "You can't keep him shut up in here for ever, it's not good for him."

"If I did take him to your place, would you promise not to let her get him?" There were tears glistening in his eyes, and he looked ready to drop.

"We promise," I said. "Cross our hearts and hope to die. He'd be safe with us."

Joe fiddled with his finger-nails, scraping the dirt from under his thumb. I felt a trickle of sweat run down my back. It was so hot.

"Maybe," he said, rubbing his hand over his temples. "Just maybe."

"You've got to get help." Ross was insistent. "The bleeding's started again, and he's losing far too much blood." Ross held a pressure pad over Blake's arm, but it soon turned bright red. "I mean it Joe, he needs help."

Blake's face had gone grey, his breathing was shallow and irregular.

"OK, OK, I'll go." Joe finally saw sense. He was running his hand through his hair, his eyes bulging. "I'll go to the chemist's, get some pain-killers."

"That won't do any good," Ross retorted.

"Well it will just have to do."

Nothing we could say would change his mind.

"Just be grateful I'm doing something, OK?"

He was panicking now, unable to cope with the situation, squirming at the sight of blood. And that's when he made a mistake. "I'm going to lock the door. If you make any attempt to escape . . ." He thrust the gun in my direction but he did not tie us up again.

"Just go Joe, hurry." Ross pulled a cushion off the settee and placed it under Blake's head.

The door slammed shut and the key turned in the lock. It was a few minutes before we heard a car engine start up.

"Right Mel, quick – try that door over there." Ross was totally in charge; I was a nervous wreck.

"It's locked," I screamed. "It's locked."

"Don't panic, is the key still in?"

I closed one eye and peered through the hole. "No, it's not, I can see right through. It looks like some kind of store-room."

"OK, now try the window, if that's locked, try and find some wire, anything, a coat hanger. What about that flower arrangement over there?"

The window wouldn't open. "We can't smash it," Ross said. "The glass would fall back on Snowy, besides, it's double glazed, it's too thick."

"There's no wire!" I threw some dried flowers on the floor.

"Come on, think, think, something to pick that lock . . ."

"My hair grip!" I suddenly remembered that I'd pinned back my fringe before we left Hollywell because it was so hot. The grip was still there, half hanging on a clump of blond hair. "I've got it!"

"Just keep calm." Ross was talking me through picking the lock. "Don't panic, just keep twiddling."

"But it's not doing any good." My hand was shaking like a leaf.

"You come and mind Blake and I'll have a go," Ross offered.

Something clicked. "It's worked!" I grabbed hold of the door handle and it swung open.

Ross was right behind me. "Come on, we haven't got much time."

Inside was a load of piled-up furniture. It wasn't a very big room and the first serious disappointment was the lack of window.

"The skylight." Ross pointed to the ceiling. "It's the only way."

We pulled out a table and piled up some boxes on top. All the time I was straining to hear the noise of a car engine. The nearest chemist was six miles away. It wouldn't take that long. What if he changed his mind, what if he came back early?

"Mel, you've got to do it, you're the only one small enough."

I looked up at the skylight with a feeling of dread.

"What about Blake?"

"He's OK, he's holding the pressure pad himself."

"Wouldn't you be better going? You can run faster than me."

"No way. I'm not leaving you here for when he gets back. There's no telling what he might do."

"But Ross . . ."

"Don't think about it, just fetch help!"

I clung on to his hand, my big brother, my safety net, the one person who was always there for me.

"Be careful," I said, "big brothers aren't that easy to replace."

"Come on, I'll give you a leg up."

I scrabbled up the boxes, ignoring my aching muscles and concentrating on keeping my balance and unscrewing the metal lock inside the skylight. It was quite straightforward; luckily it wasn't rusted up. I pushed hard and the whole thing creaked open.

The waft of fresh air was wonderful but I didn't have time to enjoy it. I heaved myself up, straining my arms, grasping, scratching, desperate to get a foothold. One shoulder was through, then the other. I was looking out at a flat roof.

"Good luck," Ross shouted, but I was too out of breath to answer. I was on my own now – it was all down to me.

I had to keep a clear head. The flat roof was a reasonable size, it looked as if it was an extension of the main house. It was still pretty high up though.

My head was swimming when I looked down at the ground. There was no way I could jump. The only chance was the drainpipe, but I was terrified of heights. I'd never even climbed a tree, let alone shinned down a drainpipe.

The thought of Ross and Blake still locked in the house was enough to send me down the metal pipe. "Dear God, let this work out," I prayed. If it came away from the wall I'd be done for.

My hands were sweating so much I didn't think I'd be able to keep a grip. I banged my knee as I swivelled round trying to get a hold with my ankles. The pain made my eyes water. "Come on Mel, you can do it," I urged myself on.

I slid down, a foot at a time. That's when I noticed the red burn marks round my wrists. It hadn't been a bad dream. Somewhere a dog barked in the distance. I could hear the church clock chiming. It was normality and it gave me the strength to carry on. The relief when my feet touched the grass was incredible. But there was no time to lose. The quickest way home was over the fields. If I went down the drive and out on to the road I might run into Joe and that didn't bear thinking about.

I set off across the lawn, scuffing across mole-hills, racing as if I was in the eight hundred metres, not daring to look back.

I scrambled across a metal gate and then flew through a field of meadow hay, the long stalks whipping at my bare legs. But I didn't feel it, the pain inside my head was far greater. I had to get to Hollywell.

Everything looked deserted as I came on to our land. Boris and Dancer were standing under the chestnut tree scratching each other's withers. There were no cars in the yard, nobody in sight.

"Trevor! Sarah!" My lungs were rasping as if

I'd got asthma. My head was pounding with pumping blood. "Somebody! Somewhere!"

Jigsaw was sitting in the yard trying to catch flies on his tummy. I had to force back the tears – I'd thought I'd never see him again.

"Mel!" There was no mistaking the voice. It was Trevor.

"Trevor! Trevor!" He came out of Colorado's stable carrying the grooming box which he promptly dropped on the concrete. Hoof oil leaked out all over the body brushes. But I didn't care because he was running towards me, catching me in his arms, hugging me like a sumo wrestler, kissing me non-stop, on the hair, on my cheeks, as if any minute I'd vanish in a puff of smoke.

"Just look at you." He held both my hands and stared into my face in shock. Heaven knows what I must have looked like, I can only guess.

"There's no time," I croaked. "Ross, Blake, the gun . . ." My voice disappeared altogether, I was just gasping for air.

"What is it, Mel? Where are they?"

"The, the R-Rectory!" My knees were buckling and Trevor had to hold me up.

Mrs Mac appeared at the back door with the

bald man in a suit. Just seeing the suit freaked me out. I thought it was Joe.

"Ring the police and call an ambulance," Trevor was telling Mrs Mac. "Get them to the Old Rectory as fast as poss. Tell them there's an armed man there."

"Derek, get your car!"

"I'm going with you!" I wasn't going to stay behind now, not after I'd come this far.

We leapt into Derek's car and he turned the ignition key. The dry, grating cough of the engine was the final straw.

"I don't believe it," said Derek. "This can't be happening."

"Quick, out, we'll go in Sarah's." Trevor was out of the car and pulling back the barn doors before I could speak.

The bright red MG roared out of the barn in a cloud of smoke.

"Come on, jump in," yelled Trevor.

"But we can't take this, it's not finished," I protested.

The sports car was Sarah's engagement present from James, and Trevor was doing it up. At the moment it had no exhaust and no bumpers.

"It's a life or death situation," Trevor shouted. "Now, come on."

I couldn't argue with that. We had to get back to the Rectory before Joe. I calculated it would take him twenty minutes to get to the chemist's and back, half an hour if he hit heavy traffic. It had taken no more than ten minutes to run from the Rectory to Hollywell, we were still in with a chance.

Trevor put his foot down and we zoomed off down the drive.

"I only hope you've fixed the brakes," I shouted, the wind whipping my hair right across my face.

Derek said he didn't have that problem, hair he meant, and I wondered how we could be having such light conversation at a time like this. But Sarah always said in tough times you could either laugh or cry. I only wished I could feel something. At the moment I was numb with shock. I felt as if all this was happening to someone else.

We hurtled down the main village High Street at fifty miles an hour. People were stopping and staring – one lady dropped all her groceries. I had to admit, we must have looked a peculiar sight.

Trevor took a corner practically on two wheels. The noise coming from underneath the car was more fitting of a juggernaut. The trees in full bloom blocked our view. I couldn't see a thing. All I noticed was a grey squirrel scampering across the road directly in front of us. Trevor swerved and we missed it by inches.

The green Land Rover was upon us before we knew it.

We were just approaching the Rectory. The Land Rover was coming from the other direction. It slowed down and switched on its right indicator. It was a full ten seconds before my brain swivelled into gear.

"That's him," I shrieked. *"That's Joe!"*

Chapter Seven

He didn't recognize me.

He was so busy concentrating on the road ahead that he didn't see me bouncing around in the back of the MG.

Not until it was too late.

Trevor had always had the ability to think fast, now he made a split second decision.

We were on the left side of the road nearest the Rectory. Joe was on the opposite side about to turn in. Without any warning Trevor slammed down the accelerator and we shot forward.

"Trevor!" I screamed.

I don't think he meant to crash the car. But then I don't think he expected Joe to deliberately ram into us.

"How the hell . . .?" Joe leapt out of the Land Rover with his eyes on me and me alone. It gave Trevor and Derek just enough time to get the upper hand.

And they didn't waste a second. Trevor charged

at Joe like a bull, slamming him back against the Land Rover bonnet. Derek whipped round to the driver's door, seizing the shotgun.

The police sirens were wailing at us from all directions.

"It's all over, matey, just give in peacefully." Trevor relinquished his arm-hold.

"You're a maniac," Joe gasped, badly winded, bending over double.

"You're under arrest." Two police officers moved in. "You do not have to say anything . . ." They were reading him his rights.

"But you can't arrest me! Who's going to look after Snowy?"

Joe was frog-marched off to a police car, his head cast down, his shoulders slumped. Just once he turned round and stared at me: dull, lonely eyes, and I almost felt sorry for him.

Sarah's car was a mess. The whole front wing was smashed in, crumpled like corrugated cardboard. It only took a few minutes to push it out of the way so that an ambulance could get past. All I was interested in was Blake and Ross. I was running blindly up the drive. A policewoman grabbed at my arm but I shook her off. I had to get to Blake.

"Mel!" It was Trevor's voice behind me.

The blue lights of the ambulance flashed round and round.

"Blake!" I shouted. He was there, coming down the steps from the front door. Safe, alive, still in one piece. Ross was at his side. "Blake!" He grinned a watery grin back at me, and one of the paramedics opened the ambulance door. "He is going to be all right, isn't he?" Tears were welling up inside me now, burning to escape.

"Mel!" Sarah appeared from nowhere, her arms enfolding me just when I needed her most. Her mascara had run and her cheeks were wet. "Thank God you're all right," she said. And I sobbed into her shoulders: it was as if a dam had just burst.

"She's in shock, it's only to be expected." At the hospital the doctor was looking down at me with a friendly face and a warm smile.

We had been told that Blake would have to stay in hospital for a few days. "But what if he's got an infection?" I said, terrified at the mention of blood-poisoning.

Sarah squeezed my hand and said it would be all right. Ross came back from the drinks machine with three cups of insipid cold tea. "The only thing we can do is go home and rest," he said, sensibly.

I knew it made sense, but I couldn't bear the idea of leaving Blake.

"He's asleep, it's what he would want," Sarah insisted.

She looked so tired, the agony of the last twenty-four hours showed on every line of her face: the not knowing, the uncertainty must have been terrible. When I managed to escape back to Hollywell she had been out in the car searching with James. They had been out all night. It was Mrs Mac who told her about the Rectory; car phones were the best thing that were ever invented.

Ross took my arm, saying, "Come on sis, let's hit the road."

Hollywell was cast in the warm glow of the sunset as we turned up the drive. Everything appeared as normal, only the empty stable next to Sally was now occupied. Two white ears protruded over the top of the door.

James had brought Snowy back to Hollywell and settled him into our medical unit, checking him over and taking a blood sample. "He needs an operation on his near hind," he told us later in the kitchen. "Apart from that he's in fine fettle." The kettle was already boiling on the Aga that James had recently fixed.

I collapsed in a chair and Oscar immediately sprung on to my knee, purring in a deep baritone.

"The man needs locking up," Sarah said, fighting off exhaustion. "To think what might have happened . . ."

"I don't think he's a particularly bad person," I said. "He's just mixed up. He loves Snowy, that must count for something."

Snowy was finding the whole experience of being in a stable both novel and bizarre. He kept wandering around, sniffing at the manger, the walls, even the haynet, as if it was all rather too much for him. James said he'd given him a bran mash and that he'd soon settle in.

"I hope we can keep him," said Katie. "He's so sweet and cuddly and he's the first donkey we've had."

She insisted on taking me out to the orchard where she and Hazel had erected a bat box on one of the apple trees.

"That reminds me," I said. "Where's Hazel?"

"We don't know," Katie answered in a low voice. "She went off to see that Beaumont woman and we've not seen her since."

"Oh," I said, feeling the rough bark of one of

74

the apple trees and thinking how it would be there probably long after all of us. I was so tired I didn't have the energy to worry about Hazel.

Back in the kitchen, Mrs Mac was cutting a portion of her apple crumble and drowning it in fresh cream. I'd suddenly developed a craving for her home-made special. It represented safety and security and it was just what I needed. I didn't think I'd ever be able to face baked beans or porridge ever again.

"Sometimes it helps to talk about it, you know," Sarah knelt down, looking me straight in the eye, full of concern.

But I didn't want to talk about it. I didn't want to dwell on the worst ordeal of our lives. It had left me ragged, empty and frightened, and I just wanted to put it all behind me.

"I – I thought I was going to lose them both," I said.

"I know," Sarah took hold of my hand, pressing it to her face. "I know."

I woke up at six o'clock the next morning with bells clanging in my head. Only it wasn't bells at all – as soon as I'd got my senses together I realized it was a series of massive "e-yore"s which threatened to wake up the whole neighbourhood, if not the entire county.

"Snowy!" I pushed up the window and felt like lobbing a book at him. He momentarily stopped and stared at me, an "e-yore" strangled in his throat, and then he started again with renewed gusto, his jaws open, his ears pricked forward.

"What's going on?" Katie stumbled into my bedroom in her pyjamas looking like a sleep-walker in a horror film. "It's only ten past six!" she squawked.

Sarah said we might as well all get up and decided that a good home-cooked breakfast was just what we needed. Katie went off to collect the eggs and I sorted out Snowy who had not only finished off his hay, but most of the clean straw in the stable as well.

"We might have to put him on woodshavings," I said to Ross who was still yawning.

Straw tended to blow horses up and make them cough. We'd never had a bed eater before.

Snowy grinned wickedly and his whole head disappeared into a bucket of coarse mix.

"I think this little fella's a bit of a character," I

said, fighting desperately to hold on to the bucket handle.

"You and me both," Ross grinned. "He's definitely starting to find his feet."

After I'd cleaned him up – he'd got pieces of straw stuck all over him, even in his ears of all places – I moved over to Colorado who looked uptight and on edge. He kept watching the back door as if Blake would appear at any minute and I noticed his bed had been trampled down where he'd marched round and round in a circle.

"Poor lad," I breathed into his nostrils. "He'll be back, he hasn't left you."

How do you tell a horse that his master has been shot and is in hospital but he's going to be all right? Colorado just stared past me uncomprehendingly, and I tried to send him telepathic messages but it didn't work.

Trevor came out with his purple hair stuck up like Snowy's mane and his jumper on back to front. "Nobody said anything about six o'clock starts," he grinned, adding that he'd collect the haynets if I did the water buckets.

It was a glorious sunny morning and the wood-pigeons were cooing nineteen to the dozen and a cuckoo was trying to compete somewhere over in the woods. I was already feeling ten times better. I seemed to be viewing everything through fresh eyes, it really was good to be alive.

"Mel come on, fetch Trevor."

Ross loaded my plate with everything from mushrooms to scrambled eggs and crispy bacon. Jigsaw got told off for slobbering at the table, and Sarah said she was way behind on her novel and that the typewriter was on the blink.

Everything had clicked back into normality and it was as if Ross and I had never been tied up and gagged in a deserted house by a madman. The peace didn't last for long. By nine o'clock the police were back on the doorstep, wanting to ask more questions even though we'd told them every little detail the night before. Roddy wanted to cover the story with me giving my own personal account but I told him quite emphatically that Ross was the hero, not me. Without him I'd have gone to pieces. The local television stations were on the phone wanting to put us on film but Sarah was as protective as a bodyguard and told them we were in no fit state to talk. Trevor even had to chase a photographer down the drive who was trying to climb up one of our trees to get a better view.

"Wouldn't it be lovely to have a quiet, uneventful week." I said to Ross, swiping at a midge which had just landed on my neck.

"No chance of that at Hollywell," he said. "You'd have to book tickets for Timbuctoo to get away from it all."

We were intent on visiting Blake. Sarah had rung the hospital and his condition was stable. We were supposed to be there two hours ago, but Walter, our mule, had escaped and pulled back the bolt on Snowy's stable. The two of them had sloped off when we weren't looking, and we found them munching runner beans in Mrs White's garden and drinking out of the fish pond. It's lucky that Mrs White was a friend, and even more lucky that the goldfish didn't have heart attacks.

We arrived at the hospital hot and bothered and I nearly freaked out when I saw Blake's bed empty with the sheets pulled back.

"It's OK, he's in the day room," a nurse shouted across, carrying a bedpan which made me squirm.

The day room was bright and breezy with a huge television and chairs lining the walls. Blake was talking to two old ladies, one who was discussing her back pain and the other complaining about gout. They looked as if they were in seventh heaven.

"Ooh, what a lovely young man," one of them said, obviously besotted with Blake.

"This is Ethel and this is Margaret." Blake introduced us, looking amused and not nearly as washed out as the night before.

Katie and Ross overloaded him with everything from grapes and chocolates to magazines and a Dick Francis thriller.

"I think I've had enough thrills to last me a lifetime," he said, plucking off a grape and sticking it in Katie's mouth.

Sarah said she thought we ought to take everything back to the ward so we left Ethel and Margaret with a packet of coffee creams and went down the corridor. We must have looked more like a coach party than hospital visitors.

The only person missing was Trevor. He had insisted on waiting in the canteen. His last run-in with Blake over the headcollar hadn't been very pleasant and he didn't know how to face him. I told him he was being stupid, but he wouldn't listen.

"How's Colorado?" was one of Blake's first questions. "And what about Snowy?"

"What about Downing Street?" Sarah said,

putting her hand up to Blake's forehead to check his temperature, and pulling down his eyes as if he were a horse.

"I'll be fit enough," Blake touched at his bandaged arm. "And if I'm not you'll just have to go without me."

"But . . ."

"The petition's the most important thing," he said. "The show must go on."

"He's right," Ross said. "We've got to get that petition to Downing Street, there are thousands of horses out there relying on us."

"Hear, hear," Katie shrieked, and then nearly choked on a Walnut Whip.

"Can you keep the noise down?" A matron strutted past looking severe. "There are patients sleeping in here."

Someone at the top of the ward was snoring so loudly I thought it would take a bomb to wake them up.

"What shall we do with Colorado?" Sarah whispered.

Trevor was behind us before we even realized.

"Listen mate," he said, scratching his head and looking embarrassed.

"It's all right," Blake butted in, "let's call it

quits, and for God's sake help me eat some of these chocolates."

We drove back from the hospital feeling a lot better and confident that Blake was going to be all right, although it would be a while before he was riding again.

"Somebody had better tell Mr Sullivan," Ross said.

Mr Sullivan was Blake's sponsor and he'd supported him through thick and thin for the last year. I only hoped his patience hadn't run out. In show-jumping the expense was colossal and the rewards few and far between.

We were all taken by surprise when we saw the car and pony trailer in the drive.

"What's going on?" Ross was suddenly serious.

I didn't have a clue but something told me it wasn't good.

"My name's Mrs Wilson." A stringy-looking woman approached us with two kids. "Mrs Joe Wilson."

"Oh." We hadn't expected this.

"I can't say how sorry I am about ..." she broke off, fumbling for words. "Anyway, the thing is ..."

"You're here for Snowy." Sarah took the words right out of her mouth.

"Yes, I am."

"But you can't, he's ours," Katie was devastated.

"No, love, it was good of you to look after him but we're going to take him home now. He belongs to Charlotte and Emily."

The two kids shuffled their feet and looked as if they couldn't care less one way or another.

"Yes, of course," Sarah said, and I couldn't believe what I was hearing.

"We've got no choice," she hissed when Mrs Wilson had gone across to Snowy's stable. "He's not an ill-treated animal, he's not neglected. She's every right to take him back."

This was the last thing we needed. I put my arm round Katie's shoulders, who was trembling.

Snowy pottered out of the stable behind Mrs Wilson wondering what on earth was going on.

Sarah explained about his leg.

"No way, he's not having an operation, I'm not wasting good money on that, it always goes back into place."

"But, Mrs Wilson—" Sarah began.

"I've made up my mind," the woman butted in.

"If he doesn't have it sorted out he'll develop arthritis, is that what you want?" Sarah retorted.

"We'll cross that bridge when we come to it, now come on, I haven't got all day." Mrs Wilson was not to be convinced.

We coaxed Snowy up the ramp. Walter banged frantically on his stable door wanting to follow his new friend, but for once he couldn't have his own way. Snowy looked across at him with sad bewildered eyes. I tied his leadrope to the ring and rubbed my hand through his stubby mane. "Look after yourself little fella."

Katie clung on to my hand as the ramp thudded shut.

"But I don't want a donkey, I want a video game," Emily blurted out.

But it didn't do any good. Mrs Wilson was not going to change her mind.

"I hate her!" Katie screeched as the trailer rattled down the drive. "I hate her, I hate her." Hot tears bubbled over her cheeks, and she ran full tilt towards the house.

"Leave her," Sarah said to Trevor. "Let her be."

*

The phone rang as we were having a cup of tea.

"It's Jennifer Beaumont," Ross came through. "She wants to speak to you, Sarah."

Chapter Eight

"But that's bribery," Ross was gobsmacked.

We were all discussing Sarah's phone conversation with "Bo" Beaumont, outraged at what had been said.

"We should have taped her conversation, put bugs in the plant pots, that kind of thing," Katie said.

"I don't believe the cheek of the woman." Sarah flopped down in the deck-chair which had somehow found its way into the kitchen.

Katie grabbed some chocolate eggs from the fridge and started gnawing on one like a squirrel. I did the same. Heaven knows we needed something.

Boot-faced Beaumont, as Trevor called her, had just offered Sarah five hundred pounds to drop the campaign to save Arnie's life.

"What kind of people does she think we are?" Sarah steamed.

"Can't we report her?" Katie broke off some chocolate for Jigsaw.

"As usual we don't have a shred of evidence." Ross was absolutely right.

"If the dressage selectors knew about this . . ."

"But don't you see," Sarah said, standing up, "we've got her on the run. She's seriously rattled. All we've got to do now is put on more pressure."

Apparently Bo had been inundated with irate phone calls after the article in the paper. She'd had to take the phone off the hook, and when Sarah told her we hadn't even started on the national papers, she went through the roof.

"The bad news is she hasn't seen Hazel. In fact she thought she was here."

"Well if she's not at Somerset Stables, where is she?" I was beginning to get seriously worried.

"That girl's in such an emotional mess she's capable of anything." Sarah was right, I had to agree.

"Oh my God!" Ross looked through the window down the drive where a pick-up truck was hauling the red MG sports car behind it like a limp dog. "Now keep calm Sarah, it's not as bad as it looks . . ."

But it was – even worse in fact. The whole right wing was a crumpled heap. The wing mirror hung broken and dejected, and the paintwork was just a criss-cross of scratches.

"Oh dear," Trevor murmured.

"Do you honestly think I'm bothered about the car?" Sarah squeaked. "It's you lot that are most important for me – a car can be replaced . . ."

"I can rebuild her Mrs F, I know I can," Trevor offered.

"Yes, Trevor, whatever you say," Sarah sighed.

"All it needs is some expertise and some spare parts," Trevor persisted.

I couldn't help wondering for the zillionth time how we could have been so wrong about Trevor. He was, as Katie put it, a forty carat dude and totally indispensable.

The car wasn't the only black spot. Sarah finally decided to open a backlog of mail which started with a monstrous overdue bill from the blacksmith and finished with a letter from Maxwell Curtis, or rather his secretary, beginning: "I am sorry to inform you . . ." He didn't want anything to do with our campaign.

"Who does he think he is?" I barked, feeling quite put out.

"Well, we don't need him." Sarah tore up the letter and sent it flying into the foot bin alongside last night's potato peelings.

"I think it's time Maxi Crowface and I had a little chat," Trevor said, a thunderstorm brewing across his face. But he didn't get a chance to elaborate.

An unexpected phone call threw us into such pandemonium that Sarah had to sit down with the dishcloth over her forehead and I just wanted to silently scream. Dominic, the producer of the Saturday morning children's programme, *The Breakfast Bunch* had just thrown a spanner in the works; he'd rearranged our plans completely. *The Breakfast Bunch* were going to film us handing in our petition which was going to be shown in September along with an update on the sanctuary. This was a real coup for Hollywell Stables – most of the viewers had become avid supporters and it would give us a chance to promote the Fan Club and to show off our new range of pencil cases and bags.

The problem was, Dom's boss was insisting he jet off to Florida to interview a pop band at the end of the week. So they'd come up with an alternative plan – we were to go to Downing Street tomorrow!

"Do tell me he's joking!" Sarah groaned.

But according to Dom it would be in our favour. He'd managed to talk one of the big feature writers from a daily paper into covering the story, and Dom insisted he might have an extra surprise up his sleeve.

"Well that's that then," Sarah said. "We must do as Master Dom commands!"

"I think we'd better start packing," said Ross.

Mrs Mac's office was a mountain of boxes. Each one contained thousands of signatures and had to be packed into the horsebox. It's a shame we hadn't reached the million target but maybe we'd been just too ambitious, there was nothing we could do about it now.

Trevor and Ross agreed to load the horsebox while Katie and I made a start on Colorado and Queenie. We had to get them gleaming like conkers, which wasn't easy when the weather was tropical, and sweat was running off my face like a stream.

"We're going to have a thunderstorm," I predicted.

"You've been saying that for weeks," Katie bantered, banging the curry comb against the wall, leaving a dusty imprint.

Queenie nodded her head up and down. I didn't know whether she was agreeing with me or Katie. Small, fluffy clouds drifted across a clear blue sky. Maybe I had got it wrong after all.

"Ouch!" I yelled, as Queenie plonked a hoof on my left foot.

"Serves you right for wearing sandals instead of jodphur boots," Katie said in her know-it-all voice.

"I wonder what this surprise is that Dom's got lined up." I had to admit, I was intrigued.

"I've told you," Katie said, "we're going to meet the Prime Minister."

"Oh yeah, pull the other one, it's got bells on," I sneered.

"Mel, you're such a cynic," Katie retorted.

"Hey, watch it," I yelled as she squirted fly spray on to Queenie's head, only she missed and it went all over my hair.

"No flies on you, big sis," she joked, and I swiped her across the legs with the stable rubber.

"It's unbelievable." Mrs Mac was thrown into a state of near delirium. "How can Dom do this to me?"

We'd sent her into the house as soon as she'd arrived, to make up some orange squash, only she'd left the door open, and now we were chasing Sarah's hens out of the kitchen. One of the oldest, a mangy cockerel, had plonked itself on Mrs Mac's new cotton cardigan.

"If I didn't know better I'd swear he was laying an egg." Mrs Mac looked as if she was going to cry.

"When the going gets tough, the tough get going," said Sarah, vaguely, wandering in from her study, sucking an ice-cream.

"There's no problem," Ross gasped, complaining that his arms felt six inches longer after carrying the boxes. "Just stay cool, hang loose."

Derek, the insurance man, arrived in the yard looking hot and stuffy, with his shirt sticking to his back.

"At least his head must be cool," Katie said, referring to his baldness. And this time I really did clip her behind the ear.

"What does he want?" I said to Trevor when Derek had been in conference with Sarah for nearly an hour. I'd tried listening at the door but Sarah had sprung me and booted me out.

"Beats me," Trevor grunted. "Maybe he's trying to sell insurance. One thing's for sure, he doesn't give up easily – this is his third visit."

Mrs Mac looked frantic as she scooted Oscar

off the ironing board and started ironing my special brick-red Hollywell T-shirt until it could have stood up by itself.

"For tomorrow," she said. "And don't dirty it."

I gave her a weak smile and then the study door slammed shut and we all tried to look busy. I buried my head in Katie's pony magazine and Ross started whistling.

"Don't even think of asking," Sarah said. "I'm sworn to secrecy, I've given my word."

"It never crossed our minds," Ross blatantly lied, as Derek's car turned out of the drive.

"It must be something important though," Katie whispered. "Did you see how she kissed his bald head?"

Colorado's white bits ended up so white I felt like entering him for a washing powder advert. Even though I say it myself, both Queenie and Colorado looked radiant, fit for the Queen, never mind the Prime Minister.

I was just finishing off polishing the bridles, picking out the dirt from the buckle holes with a matchstick just like Blake had shown me... Blake: that was a huge disappointment. The doctor had said Blake was in no fit state to go to

London. He had to stay in hospital another twenty-four hours. At this rate I'd never get to see him.

By late evening we thought we were ready. The horsebox was packed, phone calls made. Sarah had made a list of things to do: diesel at the first garage; tell James to pay the milkman; leave an extra bale of hay in the field. We were all sorted. We spent the rest of the night picking faults in an eventing video and devouring pizza and popcorn.

"It's all going too well." Sarah pushed back the foot stool. "Something's bound to go wrong, it always does."

We thought she was just being paranoid. But we should have known better.

It was one o'clock in the morning when the phone rang and I was still awake, dreaming about Prime Ministers and romantic summer evenings. I was the first to reach the phone.

It was Hazel. She was in a phone box and she sounded desperate. She told me where she was, and then the pips started going. All I caught was her saying, "I've done something really stupid . . ."

Chapter Nine

The rain poured down in slanting sheets. A crack of lightning lit up the blackened sky, and I shivered inside as if someone had just walked over my grave.

"Hazel?" I called out. The torchlight flickered over some rough scrub.

"Are you sure this is where she said she was?" Sarah came up beside me, rain sliding off the brim of her sou'wester.

"Look – over there," Ross scrambled down a bank, taking the torch with him and plunging us into instant darkness.

"Ross!" I stumbled forward, tripping over the surcingle which surrounded the weatherproof rug I was carrying, and cringing as warm rain drops funnelled their way down my neck and back. It was a first class storm, just as I'd predicted.

Sarah took my elbow and we half slithered, half tumbled down the steep slope, a clump of nettles biting into my hand as I groped for extra balance.

"There!" Ross held the torch still and I could vaguely make out the old railway tunnel and the figure waving frantically at its entrance.

"We're over here!" The voice echoed for ages, eerie and high pitched. It was Hazel. "Before you say anything, I know it was a crazy thing to do."

Arnie stood under the huge arch looking like a drowned rat with his forelock stuck to his ears and his tail clamped down between his hindlegs. I think he would have given anything to be back in his warm stable with a full haynet and a dry bed and I didn't blame him.

"You certainly pick your nights," Ross said, casting the torch over Arnie's near fetlock which was starting to swell.

"Hazel, what on earth did you think you were doing?"

We were a mile from Somerset Stables, and Hazel explained how she couldn't bear leaving Arnie with Bo for a second longer. She'd been camping rough on the edge of a wood overlooking the Beaumont land, determined to keep watch, a pair of binoculars trained on his stable. The other grooms had gone into town to a nightclub; Bo and her man friend were at a dinner party. There was only the housekeeper on the premises – it was too good an opportunity to miss.

"I'd led him out of the stable before I'd even thought what I was going to do with him." She was visibly shivering from head to foot and Ross took off his jacket and wrapped it round her shoulders. "And then it started thundering . . . Arnie hates thunder, it scares him to death."

I was beginning to get the picture. "You poor old boy." I rubbed at his ears which were cold and wet and Ross slung the rug over his hindquarters.

"You see what I mean?" Hazel said.

Arnie's head was practically between his knees and he was trembling even more than Hazel. If it hadn't been so serious it would have been comical. He was almost trying to hide behind us all as a roll of thunder rattled ominously over the tunnel. If he could have leapt into Hazel's arms I think he would have done.

"It's OK boy, it's not going to hurt you."

"We've got to get him out of here." Sarah stated the obvious. "This rain, and his arthritis – he soon won't be able to walk."

Hazel's bottom lip quivered and I could almost feel the agony she was going through. "I would have done the same thing in your shoes," I said, trying to make her feel better.

I could still remember vividly when Blake and I had kidnapped Colorado and hidden him in the cow shed at the bottom of the field. It was stupid and irrational but when you're desperate you do anything.

"We can't go breaking the law," Sarah said, looking out at the driving rain. "There's only one course of action—"

"But I thought you'd take him back to Hollywell?" Hazel's voice had almost become a screech.

I was pretty speechless myself.

"It's got to be as if nobody knew this happened," Sarah insisted. "We've got to take him back to Somerset Stables."

We plodded along a bridlepath, Sarah, Ross, Hazel and myself, and Arnie crawling along looking as if the sky was going to fall on his head at any minute.

"If only it would stop thundering," Hazel shuddered.

"At least we're all wearing rubber wellies," Ross said as lightning lit up the sky.

"And just think what this rain will do for the grass." I tried to make conversation but it fell flat.

"It's not doing much for Arnie's nerves," Hazel groaned as Arnie caught sight of a fluttering crisp bag and carried on as if it was a fire-breathing dragon.

Somerset Stables was just at the bottom of the dip; all we had to do was cross a road and we could go in the back way through the dressage arenas and into the stable yard. We passed the telephone box where Hazel had contacted us and where she said Arnie had nearly strangled himself trying to get in the door.

"Oh no." Hazel stopped dead in her tracks.

The whole of Somerset Stables was lit up and a car was parked at an angle across the drive.

"They're back." Hazel's voice was a whimper. "Angela said they were staying out all night. What are we going to do? They're back!"

Panic set in like a suffocating fog. We had to get Arnie into his stable.

"It might not be as bad as it looks," Sarah said, taking charge. "Hazel, you said they don't check the stables last thing at night?"

"That's right, they usually just go straight to bed. It's the grooms' job to check the horses."

"But they're not here, only Bo doesn't know that."

"Exactly."

"OK, this is what we'll do." Sarah took off her yellow sou'wester, shaking off the streams of water and stuffing it in her pocket. She said it was too bright and she might get noticed. "Hazel and I will take Arnie, Ross will keep watch, and you, Mel, will go up to the front door and distract them."

"You've got to be joking!" I nearly twisted my ankle in a rut as I swivelled round in shock. My voice-box seemed to have dried up to sawdust.

"Mel, it's the only way. You can do it, I know you can."

"But why me, why not Ross?"

"Because you can talk better, and besides, you've got a better imagination."

"What for?"

"For whatever you're going to tell them." Sarah said, unhelpfully.

Oh, great, this was all I needed. I was beginning to think Arnie would have been better off at Hollywell after all, even if it did mean breaking the law.

The front door was ivory white with a doorbell that chimed like a cathedral and dogs that barked like the Hound of the Baskervilles. I wanted to run for it, but that wouldn't be enough of a distraction – I had to keep them talking. Besides, my legs were rooted to the spot.

Jennifer Beaumont opened the door, looking every inch a charismatic star in a black velvet dress and diamanté jewellery. She was holding a brandy glass, and unless it was my imagination, swaying slightly in her high heels.

"Yes, hello?" She looked at me enquiringly.

Anybody would be shocked to see a bedraggled teenage girl on the doorstep at two in the morning. Especially someone from Hollywell Stables who was more likely to put a poison pen letter through the letterbox than ask to come in.

"I don't understand, what's going on?" Her clipped, staccato voice sounded nervous. I think she was actually apprehensive of me.

A fleet of sooty black labradors hurled themselves round the corner and descended into the hallway, all slavering tongues and wagging tails.

"Darling, what's going on?" It was the man who'd been on the shooting stick.

I stepped inside and said it was of the utmost importance that I speak to her. I had a message.

"So why didn't she come and do her own dirty work?" Bo screwed up her face in distaste. I had to admit she was rather glamorous. "Somebody ought to have a word with that woman. Who does she think she is, telling people how to run their lives? She needs to get a grip."

"Darling, let's hear what the girl's got to say," the man said, trying to calm her down.

"Well, that's it really," I stuttered. "Just that we've decided to call off the campaign to save Arnie. Sarah wanted me to tell you straight away."

"At nearly three in the morning? Couldn't it have waited until a respectable hour?" I decided that she looked better in photos than she did in real life.

"We were coming back from an emergency call and we saw the light on." It sounded pathetically weak, but she fell for it.

"I knew she would see sense in the end. Tell her from me to stick to what she can handle: little ponies and seaside donkeys," Bo sneered.

I bit my tongue so hard it stung my eyes. I still had to buy time. "Can I have your autograph?"

Jennifer Beaumont almost smirked in surprise. "Well I don't suppose it's your fault you've got such a troublesome mother."

"She's not my mother, she's my stepmother."

Jennifer swirled out of the hallway and came

back two minutes later with a signed photograph of her riding her best horse, Solitaire.

"I hope you appreciate that," she said, opening the door.

I heard the owl hoot I'd been waiting for and raced out of the house as if the devil himself were behind me.

"We did it!" Ross hissed, lifting me off my feet in relief. "Arnie's ploughing through his haynet and you wouldn't suspect a thing."

"Apart from his muddy feet," Hazel said. "But I think I managed to wipe off the worst."

"There's only one thing to do now," Sarah said, looking completely whacked. "Let's go home."

"I promise you, Hazel, give me twenty-four hours and Arnie will be at Hollywell for good." Sarah was trying to console Hazel.

"How can you say that?" Hazel had broken down in tears as soon as we sat in the kitchen. Jigsaw was slobbering over her knees and Trevor and Katie wanted to know everything that had happened.

"I can't say exactly," Sarah stalled. "Let's just say it was vital that Arnie be in his stable tomorrow morning."

"*This* morning." Katie looked out of the window where dawn was just breaking.

Ross and I exchanged meaningful looks. There was no doubt Sarah knew more than she was letting on, but it was so unlike her to keep secrets; we were all normally so honest and open.

"I think Mrs F's got something up her sleeve." Trevor, as usual, said what he thought.

"Trevor, the milk!" Sarah leapt up to switch off the boiling milk before it ran all over the old Aga which was now her pride and joy. It was also a good way to change the subject.

Hazel looked grey and worn to a frazzle and Trevor plied her with hot cocoa and home-made cookies. She admitted that she'd been living off muesli bars and stewed tea from a flask. Camping out, even in summer, wasn't all it was cracked up to be.

"That wouldn't keep a flea going," Trevor snorted, taking a handful of cookies and demolishing them.

"You should have told us where you were," Sarah said. "We've all been worried."

"I figured you had enough of your own problems, locked up in that house – I heard it all on the radio."

Ross and I clammed up. It was something we

still didn't want to talk about. It was all shut away in the recesses of our minds, not for dwelling on.

Trevor went to fetch a towel for Hazel's wet hair and Sarah gave her a bundle of dry clothes. Oscar went flying through the air off a kitchen unit on to Ross's shoulder looking desperate for an early morning feed. I opened a tin of cat food and asked if it was really worth going to bed when we had to be up in an hour and a half?

The last time we'd been in London was to appear on *The Breakfast Bunch* and I couldn't wait to see Dom and Cassandra again in the flesh. They were completely wacky and bizarre but great fun, and they really cared about Hollywell Stables.

"I vote we stay up," Katie said, leaning back against the units and accidentally plonking her hand in Oscar's food.

"Oh no, Katie, not Snakes and Ladders." The last thing I was in the mood for was being thrashed at Snakes and Ladders by my little sister. "Let's just sit here and doze," I suggested, yawning and letting my eyelids shut. Jigsaw barked as if this was the best idea.

"Oh no," Katie said, looking in the sugar tin. "I've lost my four-leaf clover!"

We spent the next hour looking for Katie's plastic clover which went on all the big occasions, and which she had convinced us brought oodles of luck.

"Well think when you last had it," I snapped, having finished emptying the magazine rack and scouring the carpet.

"It's here." Ross held up a chewed plastic lump which he'd found in Oscar's cardboard house, but something else distracted our attention and had us all frozen to the spot.

"It can't be," I said.

"I don't believe it." Ross shook his head.

"It is!" Katie shrieked, leaping up and flinging open the back door.

Two huge white ears plunged forward and we were deafened by the loudest "e-yore" this side of a donkey farm.

"Snowy, what are you doing here?"

The poor little guy was in a terrible state. His coat was covered in burrs and was all crinkled from the storm. His nose was badly scratched and he had a deep gash down his shoulder where it looked as if he'd run into something.

"He must have escaped," I said. "He must have been wandering around all night."

Even worse, his near hind leg was fixed straight at an agonizing angle. It had happened again.

James was with us at the speed of light. "OK, little chappie, let's get you into a stable."

"I'm going to operate on his leg," James said. "There are complications – it's got to be done. And he needs stitches in that shoulder."

Snowy huddled up to my body as if he needed the contact. He looked sad and forlorn and I just wanted to hug him and tell him it was going to be all right. James rigged up some extra lighting and Trevor said he'd be the assistant and pass over the instruments.

James pulled on a pair of fine plastic gloves and said Snowy would be all right with a tranquillizer and a local anaesthetic. It was only a small operation.

Sarah was flying round the house trying to get ready and Ross and Hazel were feeding all the horses. Buckets were clanking like an army canteen and then Ross remembered someone had better warm up the horsebox, and then there were Queenie and Colorado to bandage and rug up for the journey.

Sarah came hopping out of the house in a

daffodil yellow two piece suit, with one shoe on and the other half-off and a piece of toast in her mouth.

"Mel, we've got to leave in twenty minutes."

Snowy nuzzled at my hand and I felt his nose which was all rough and grazed.

"Well then, you'll have to go without me," I said. "I'm staying here with Snowy."

Chapter Ten

"OK, Mel, hold his head," James moved forward with the scalpel. Trevor backed off looking pea-green.

"Basically all I'm going to do is cut the patella ligament inside the leg." James carried on talking as he worked. "I've never seen this condition in a donkey before."

Luckily I couldn't see anything and Snowy just stood, drowsy and well behaved, not aware of anything.

"Under normal circumstances I'd advise building up the muscle in the hindleg, that usually does the trick, but in this case . . ."

"Gee, James, I don't know how you keep your hand steady." Trevor's were trembling like a road digger.

"Here, you can start threading me that needle." James pointed to some thread in his black case.

The wound on Snowy's shoulder was open and gaping and James said he'd have to clean it up first. He took a pair of surgical scissors and moistening some cotton wool in antiseptic, he placed it inside the wound.

"That's to stop the cut hair falling in," he said. I just winced and looked the other way.

The proper word for stitching is "suturing". I couldn't believe how quick and neat James was. Trevor said he put his Granny to shame and she'd been embroidery champion at her WI club for the last ten years.

"There, all done." James snipped off the thread. "He'll be as right as rain in a few days, won't you, fella?" James patted his neck and said somebody ought to contact Mrs Wilson but we didn't have her phone number and when we rang Enquiries they said she was ex-directory.

"That's that then," Trevor said.

We settled Snowy down in the stable, the tranquillizer already wearing off. James put his things in the car and Mrs Mac arrived with a pile of cookery books and one of Sarah's romantic novels. She hadn't wanted to go to London in case Dom had caught her on film, and besides, she said, it was too hot for travelling. Her job was to horse-sit, but now we were here there was no need.

"It's a shame you had to miss the big occasion," she said.

The house was deathly quiet with just Jigsaw wandering around wondering where everybody had gone. My over-pressed, brick-red Hollywell T-shirt was still on the back of a chair.

"Snowy needed us more," I said and meant it, although I wished sometimes everything wouldn't happen at once.

"Here's somebody who needs you, too," Mrs Mac looked out of the window as a taxi pulled into the yard.

A dark-haired tall young man got out with one arm in a sling.

"Blake!" I went hysterical. "It's Blake!"

I shot out of the back door like a whippet and practically careered into his arms just as he was paying the taxi driver.

"Steady on," he grinned, looking more like the old Blake.

"But how did you get out?" I made it sound like a prison.

"Simple," he said. "I just checked out."

"But what did the doctor say?"

"I told him I'd got a better nurse here, besides I was fed up with fish, jelly and ice-cream."

111

I thumped him on his good shoulder and then told him about Snowy and Arnie and Hazel and how we'd been up all night.

Mrs Mac came outside and shook his hand, saying he needed feeding up. Trevor said he was probably going to be fussed to death and he hoped he could stand the pace. I couldn't stop grinning and didn't feel half so bad about missing the trip to London.

"Eh up, what's this?" Trevor was the first to notice the red Royal Mail parcel van coming up the drive.

"Beats me," I said, mentally checking that it wasn't anybody's birthday.

"Mrs Foster?" The parcel man looked at Mrs Mac. I signed the clipboard in Sarah's place and nearly flipped when I saw who the boxes were from – *In The Saddle*, one of the top pony magazines! They'd collected a mountain of signatures, and we hadn't known anything about it.

"You realize this pushes us over the million mark." Trevor read the letter which was attached to one of the boxes.

"It's incredible," I said, looking over his shoulder.

"It's a terrible shame." Mrs Mac dabbed at her

eyes with the tea towel. "All that work, and it arrives an hour too late."

"The cruel twist of fate." Trevor developed that glazed distant look which I knew so well. He was plotting something, no doubt about it. "I've just got to have a yarn with someone on the dog and bone," he said, meaning the telephone.

"What's he up to?" Blake whispered ten minutes later as I made him a cup of tea. James had rushed off to see a bull in distress so there was just the four of us.

"Right get your glad rags on." Trevor barged into the kitchen looking flushed. "We're going to London."

"Trevor, don't be stupid, if we set off this minute we'd still be hours late. There's no way we can get to London in time."

"Stop complaining," Trevor barked. "Anyway, we're not going by car."

"I don't see why you have to be so mysterious." Mrs Mac drove her car out of the village, Trevor in the front, Blake and I in the back. "Why can't you tell us what's going on?"

The biggest shock had been Trevor's suit. I couldn't believe it when he raced down the stairs doing up a fancy tie and white shirt and looking like the cat's whiskers. As we'd only ever seen him in extra large heavy metal T-shirts and King Kong sized boots, it was like a make-over on daytime telly, only ten times more dramatic.

"Here!" Trevor screeched and Mrs Mac slammed on the brakes.

We were parked slap bang outside the country estate of our Member of Parliament, Maxwell Curtis.

"Well, don't waste time, come on, up the drive!"

I'd never seen a house so big, or a drive so vast – it must have been acres across.

The helicopter was on the lawn, the propellers already turning.

"Glad you could make it." Maxwell Curtis strode out of the house looking confident and immaculately groomed. "I'll have to ask you to hurry, we haven't got a minute to lose."

A fleet of staff helped us carry the boxes of signatures towards the helicopter. Mrs Mac waved frantically and Trevor's hair blew up in the vacuum of air so he resembled a startled cockatoo.

"I don't believe this is happening," I mumbled, and took Blake's advice to just go with the flow.

The helicopter soared up over the patchwork of fields and my stomach flipped over, half with nerves and half with excitement. Blake held my hand and we stared out at the view of England with something amounting to patriotic pride.

"So as I was saying," Trevor shouted over to Mr Curtis who was actually doing the flying. Locked in like an insect in a bottle Mr Curtis had no choice but to listen to Trevor's never-ending spiel about the importance of improving awareness of equine welfare. Trevor successfully bent his ear from the moment of lift-off to seconds before landing.

"Look, the Houses of Parliament," Blake breathed as we hovered over London feeling like royalty. This was a journey I would never forget.

As soon as we landed, someone slid back the doors, and there was a car waiting some distance away with a chauffeur in full uniform.

"Number Ten Downing Street," Mr Curtis shouted and then climbed into an identical car parked behind.

Blake, Trevor and I piled into the back seat with the boxes in the boot for the five minute drive to Downing Street.

"All we need now is some cucumber sandwiches," Trevor joked as the car set off with barely a murmur.

"I want a full explanation and I want it now," I eyed Trevor with eagle-like intensity. "Just how did you pull this off?"

As usual he was as slippery as an eel but after five minutes in a traffic jam he told us that he had saved Maxwell Curtis's dog from being run over and that Maxwell had owed him a favour.

Mr Curtis had gone on to the House of Commons and had actually invited us back to take tea in the Members' Dining Room if we had time.

It was pandemonium. Black taxis were pushing out of queues, honking horns, trying to do U-turns; there was every type of car, and tons with foreign number plates.

"This is ridiculous. It's only just round the corner," Trevor said, pulling at his shirt collar which had turned his neck turkey red.

"Deep breathing," Blake said to me as I really started to flap.

"Blake, believe me, this is no time for meditation," I said.

The sun was getting hotter, and out on the streets people were stripping off to the bare minimum. I saw every kind of T-shirt, from holes in the back, to holes in the front and bare midriffs. I even saw one woman wandering along in what looked like her best bra.

"It's called culture," Blake grinned.

Trevor asked if we realized that we were in the middle of an international city, and where was Pall Mall and Buckingham Palace? I don't think he'd been to London before. I had to insist that we wouldn't have time to go to Madame Tussauds.

"OK, here goes," the chauffeur piped up. "Let's take the bull by the horns."

We dived down a side street, narrowly missing a powder blue Rolls-Royce, and scorched along at the rate of knots.

Blake grinned at a woman carrying a poodle into an exclusive looking veterinary clinic – she was unloading more baskets and bowls from the car than you'd find in a pet shop.

"Sure is different from the country." Trevor scratched his head, looking completely fazed.

We sailed down street after street trying to drive around the traffic until in the end I surrendered to the fact that we were going to miss the presentation.

Trevor was just about to apologize for what seemed like a good idea when I suddenly caught sight of our horsebox and Colorado in his best show rug.

"We're here," I shrieked, grabbing hold of

Blake's injured arm and causing him to wince. "We're just in time!"

There was little Queenie, her brown coat shining, and Katie holding on to her looking about to burst with pride. Sarah was flying around in her yellow suit, as fizzy as a lemon sherbet, and Hazel was frantically oiling Colorado's feet, only he wouldn't stand still and he kept barging into someone in a striped shirt.

"That's Andrew Davison," I hissed, "the top National Hunt jockey, and look over there, by the ramp, it's Daniel Lamond." I couldn't believe that so many famous people had turned up.

Sarah practically flipped her lid when she saw us running towards her. I think she thought we were a vision. "But that's brilliant!" she said. "There's a reporter from *In The Saddle* here somewhere."

Already there were loads of people milling around, cameras everywhere, tape recorders. Blake went across to Colorado who was getting more skittish by the second.

"The Minister of Agriculture should be here any minute," Sarah said, pulling out her speech and rehearsing it just one more time.

I helped Ross pull out a white board from the horsebox which we'd had specially made. It said:

"Here Are One Million Protests Against The Live Export Of Horses For Slaughter."

I'd never felt so elated as at that moment. It was the sense of achievement, the actual doing, the making a difference. It was something I couldn't describe.

"Here, hold Queenie a minute," Katie stuffed the lead rope into my hand and ran off to chat up Andrew Davison.

"The little minx," I said, under my breath, as I'd been planning to do exactly the same thing.

Queenie found some mints in my jeans pocket and I put my arm over her neck and thought how far we'd come since that night we'd found her, near to death in a scrap-yard. It seemed a lifetime ago, and now she was the best lucky mascot any sanctuary could wish for.

Sarah strutted up the ramp in her high heels, ordering Ross and Trevor to reorganize some of the cardboard boxes so that they were in better view of the cameras. On each box we'd slapped a Hollywell sticker, just for some extra publicity – you could never stop trying.

The feature writer from one of the daily papers was chasing Sarah around with a tape recorder asking meaningful questions. He'd got a pony tail and wore burgundy glasses and didn't look like a top writer at all.

I was just about to ask what had happened to Dom and Cassandra when a familiar *Breakfast Bunch* car whizzed up, screeching the tyres, and the long gazelle legs of Cassandra leapt out of the back causing a ripple of excitement. Then the rest of Cassandra followed, along with Dom who was half her size and as usual wearing the gaudiest bow tie and silk skirt anybody could find this side of the tropics. But we loved them both to death and Sarah was the first to race forward and hug Cassandra.

"Is everything fixed?" Dom fussed, organizing his own camera crew and wiping a smudge off Katie's face which she didn't appreciate in the least.

I had a word with the sound man to keep the sound boom away from Queenie and Colorado. The last time we'd had one near the horses Boris had devoured it in one go. I didn't want the film going out on telly resembling a silent movie.

"OK, get ready to roll." Dom ran a hand through his hair in typical producer style. Reporters shuffled for position as the countdown began.

Sarah wiped her hands on her skirt and prepared to knock at the door of Number Ten. Katie stuck up her thumb in a good luck sign, and I hissed at her to be careful, you never knew where the cameras were lurking.

I was so proud of Sarah, she looked so beautiful and sophisticated as she approached the huge famous door. The Minister of Agriculture seemed like a really nice guy. He posed for pictures with Sarah on the horsebox ramp in front of the boxes. Sarah said her speech word perfect, and there was just the right amount of feeling and passion without going overboard. She'd been practising in the kitchen for the last few weeks with James acting as adviser. He'd given loads of speeches on medical matters.

"Bravo," Cassandra cheered when it was all over and the cameras had stopped rolling. Everybody gave a round of applause and then there were more pictures to be taken with Queenie and Colorado. I nearly died when the whole Hollywell team had to pose. I'm sure I had my eyes closed on most of the photographs.

Colorado wouldn't stop neighing. Katie said he could probably hear the Queen's horses but I denied this as a load of rubbish. It was more likely over-excitement.

It was all an incredible success and I prayed

from the bottom of my heart that it would do some good. It was only when we'd got trapped in the lorry going across to France that we'd really discovered the conditions in which many horses were transported abroad for slaughter. It was so terrible that something had to be done and fast. Public awareness was the best approach – Sarah always said that the general public could move mountains if they really wanted to. They just had to care enough and be brought together. I wanted to say a personal big thank-you to the one million people who had signed our petition. It was fantastic.

"Penny for your thoughts," Blake said coming up to me, holding a very restless Colorado.

"You know, Blake, life really is wonderful – it's just the best!"

"You weren't saying that an hour ago when we were stuck in that traffic jam," he joked, and I couldn't help agreeing.

Reporters started to drift off and we loaded Queenie and Colorado, who were starving and tore at their haynets as if they hadn't been fed for a week.

I showed Cassandra some photographs of the Hollywell residents: Fluffy, our little Falabella, who had made an amazing recovery; Isabella, the pot-bellied pig who was now a major attraction but still getting into mischief and still as greedy as ever; Jakey, the lovely piebald cob now retired and enjoying a quiet life.

Tears were welling up in Cassandra's eyes as we reminisced on times past. It was so good to see her again. She'd always be welcome at Hollywell Stables even if she did like seaweed-tasting tea and kept trying to convert us to rabbit food and sunflower seeds.

"OK, we're on." Dom raced up, looking more excited than I'd ever seen him.

"Could somebody please tell me what's going on?" Sarah said.

Sometimes in life things change so dramatically that just when you think it can't get any better it does. I'd read in a magazine that sometimes you had to go through really bad times to enjoy the good; life was like a pendulum – and looking back over the last week I think they'd got a point.

As Sarah approached the brass knocker of Number Ten for the second time that day we were all trembling in our shoes. The whole Hollywell team was present, Blake, Trevor, even Hazel. The policeman at the door stood aside and a secretary showed us in. We stepped into a hall and my immediate thought was how small it was. I'd imagined Number Ten to be a bit like a Tardis.

"Ssssh," Sarah whispered as we were left alone in a room. Unbelievably the *Breakfast Bunch* cameras had been allowed in and Cassandra was bickering with Dom about exactly what kind of angle to aim for.

I looked around the room, which was beautiful with masses of impressive pictures on the walls. Katie and Ross flicked through some outdated magazines on a coffee table. My knees were buckling underneath me, it was almost like waiting at the dentist's but a hundred times worse.

The door opened just as I was staring at a picture of Disraeli. We were shown up a narrow staircase with endless photographs of past Prime Ministers. The camera was right behind me and I felt vaguely like Anneka Rice and became acutely aware of my bottom.

"Step inside." The lady showed us into a study.

It was dimly lit and had a lovely cosy atmosphere. The palms of my hands were sweating and my heart was hammering like ten thousand pistons. I didn't notice the man at the window, not until he turned round and looked straight at me. It was the Prime Minister!

Chapter Eleven

"We had tea with the Prime Minister!" Katie shrieked into the mobile phone. Mrs Mac was completely stuck for words at the other end.

Dom had said that it was the best film ever and Sarah was saying that Hollywell Stables had finally "arrived," although where, I couldn't quite work out.

"Did you see the way he was looking at the photographs?" My heart was still banging like mad.

"He's definitely an animal lover," Katie insisted, talking nineteen to the dozen.

We were on our way home in the horsebox, all squashed in, Trevor's jacket slung in the back of the cab and his spotted tie hung up next to some of Blake's rosettes.

Blake, Ross and Hazel were following behind with Cassandra who was going to stay at Hollywell for a couple of days. She said she had some time owing, and Dom could manage Florida by himself. Besides, she knew which place she'd rather be.

"We are the champions," Katie started to sing.

We heard Snowy braying before we reached the stables. Mrs Mac said he was as perky as a tom cat in spring and he'd taken a particular shine to her new "extra rich" recipe for flapjack. Sarah stopped off at the Bottle And Pig to buy a bottle of champagne and Cassandra went on ahead driving as if she were blasting her way along the M25. I saw Mrs White's curtains twitch and the colonel who was across the road cutting his privet hedge nearly chopped off a clump of hollyhocks.

"We're home!" Katie yelled as the diesel engine died out and we climbed down as stiff as boards.

Walter yawned over his stable door and Oscar carried on watching for mice.

"Well thanks for the welcome, gang," I said, suddenly feeling an overwhelming love for the countryside and all it represented. I couldn't live in a big city for all the tea in China – it just wouldn't be Hollywell.

The sweet fragrance of new mown grass wafted up and James appeared from the front garden with his hair stuck on end and a slick of oil across one cheek. Sarah gave him a hug and told him he smelled of elderberries and asked what he had been doing.

James ignored her and said practically the whole county was chasing her, namely Mrs Wilson and Derek who said, and he quoted, "Everything was on course – just give him the word."

What on earth did that mean?

"Oh and about the elderberries," James followed her into the house looking vague, "I thought I might try making a drop of home brew . . ."

The kitchen was full of plastic tubes and strange looking bottles and a manual on how to make wine. Sarah said he wouldn't have such a free rein when they were married and buzzed off to the hallway to use the phone.

She was on the line to Mrs Wilson for a long time. She said that Snowy had panicked when the storm began and had ploughed through a wire fence.

Cassandra made a cup of herbal tea and looked twitchy, and Katie cut out a picture of a white donkey and stuck it on the wall.

Mrs Wilson was probably at this moment going bananas that we'd operated on Snowy. It was amazing how he'd managed to find his way back here, but then they always say that equines have a mysterious sixth sense.

"Well?" Cassandra said as soon as Sarah came into the kitchen.

Sarah's face was grave. Joe was out on bail and undergoing therapy. He was quite obviously mentally unstable and this would figure largely when his case came to court. Mrs Wilson said they were selling the family house, which had a monstrous mortgage and was partly why their marriage had broken up in the first place. Joe had been cracking up under the pressure for quite some time. She was going to stand by him and give their marriage another go, not just for the sake of the kids but because she still loved him.

"And where does this leave Snowy?" I had to ask, I was bristling with tension.

"Well I hope you can stand being woken up every morning," Sarah said. "Because Mrs Wilson wants him to stay right here!"

"You're joking!" we chorused.

"No, straight up," Sarah assured us.

"You're serious?"

"Every bit."

"Yippee!" Katie shrieked and ran out to tell Snowy.

Cassandra wanted to know if they could use

Snowy for *The Breakfast Bunch*'s Christmas play and Sarah said they'd have to watch Walter didn't lead him astray in the meantime. Heaven knows what the mule would get up to next.

James thought it was seriously time for a party and what about a barbecue? Sarah said she'd invite Roddy and then of course there was Derek . . .

"Mrs Foster?" Hazel came in from outside. "You haven't forgotten about Arnie, have you?" Her face was a picture of desolation.

"I never break a promise, Hazel. I said he'd be here within twenty-four hours and he will be."

"Sarah?" James caught her elbow and frog-marched her into the study. All we could hear was a torrent of urgent whispers and then James's voice partially raised. "Just what is going on?"

"I thought we could put his water bucket in an old tyre to stop him kicking it over, and maybe some sacking on the inside of the door to stop him banging." Trevor was being innovative as ever. Snowy glared at him with beady eyes.

"I think he knows what you're talking about," I said.

"Of course he does." Katie came out of his stable. "He's a donkey, isn't he?"

Trevor finished with the idea of a swede or

sugar beet suspended on a piece of rope as a play toy, anything to stop him getting bored, and then there was a cloud of smoke from the front garden and Mrs Mac shrieking like a banshee.

"It'll be the charcoal on the barbecue that's damp," Trevor said, as a column of black smog curled its way up over the house. "Oscar's been using it as cat litter tray for the last few months."

Cassandra insisted on making up some high fibre veggie-burgers and discussed at length the nutritional value of sesame seeds on bread buns. Roddy arrived clutching a bunch of wilting carnations and promptly sat in one of the plastic chairs outside which was still harbouring a puddle from the storm.

"Oh dear," he said, plucking at his trousers.

Sarah was like a cat on hot bricks, getting more nervous by the minute. She'd changed out of the daffodil yellow suit into something cooler and was now wrestling with a tossed salad.

"I hope you know what you're doing about Arnie," I said. "Hazel will be heartbroken if it goes wrong."

"Wrong? Don't be so silly," she screeched and tossed the salad a little too intensely so that the iceburg lettuce went sailing through the air and plopped in Jigsaw's basket.

It was a beautiful evening, slants of sleepy russet sun dying out like the embers on a fire. It was warm without being overpowering and fresh and balmy after the torrential rain.

"Fancy a walk?" Blake asked, picking up a stick for Jigsaw and throwing it towards the orchard. There wasn't much we could do to help out: James was scuttling around in Sarah's frilly pinny and Cassandra was getting quite carried away with the bellows.

"A good draw, that's what it needs," she said, coughing as the smoke veered back towards her.

It was cooler among the apple trees and I took off my trainers so I could sink my bare feet into the long grass.

"It's been a dramatic week," Blake said, watching Jigsaw run on ahead, frisking around like a puppy.

"The worst," I said, pulling at a strand of my hair which had fallen loose.

"But this is nice, though."

We carried on walking, looking at the clover and the buttercups which were closing up their heads ready for the approaching night. All but the last rays of daylight had disappeared.

"I wonder what the Prime Minister would

think of this," Blake said, throwing Jigsaw's stick so it skipped and spun over the long grass.

"I think he'd think it was pretty fantastic," I said. "Maybe he'll call in one day like he said."

"Maybe."

Blake slowed down his pace so we were walking side by side.

"Listen," I suddenly said, catching his shirt sleeve. "Ssssh." There it was, a high-pitched squeak, a swoop and flutter, a black shadow. "It's a bat."

We listened intensely in the dusk, and I swore I saw more than two.

"Don't tell Katie," Blake whispered, "but there have been bats here as long as I've lived here."

"Oh," I said, and that's when he bent down and kissed my lips and bells erupted in my head and it was just like in Sarah's romantic novels, only better because this was for real.

"So where have you two been?" James grinned, shovelling blackened sausages from side to side; Cassandra was waiting for her veggie-burgers, vulture-like.

My face coloured up bright red and Blake

started to say something I couldn't hear, and that's when Sarah let out a half strangled shriek.

I turned round as if in slow motion to see a big steel grey horse bouncing up the drive with poor Derek hanging on to the lead rope for dear life.

"Do something!" he gasped as he was nearly scraped against the wall. "Help!"

"It's Arnie!" Hazel finally clunked into gear. "It's Arnie!" She put down a tub of coleslaw and leapt over a rose bed just as Arnie was about to wrap Derek round the nearest telegraph pole.

"He's all yours, love, you can have him with pleasure." Arnie butted Derek in the stomach and then proceeded to slobber all over Hazel's hair. Precariously balanced around his neck was a big red bow which had been half eaten but it was the thought that counted.

"I don't believe it," Hazel mumbled, tears welling up in her eyes. "I honestly don't believe it."

"Anyway the bottom line is that the insurance firm preferred you to take him than obtain their carcass money," Derek explained. "I talked it all over with Mrs F . . . He really is a lovely horse."

"But why all the cloak and dagger stuff?" Ross asked. "Why didn't you tell us?"

"Mainly because I didn't want Hazel building

her hopes up," Sarah explained, handing out the burgers. "It was all up in the air until a few hours ago. Jennifer Beaumont thought Derek was having him as a pet – she'll hit the roof when she finds out the truth."

"So she's still getting her ten thousand pounds?" I asked.

"Absolutely," Sarah said. "But we get to keep Arnie."

It all sounded very complicated to me. Roddy said he'd heard of this before when an insurance company paid out on a greyhound but the Managing Director fell in love with it and took it home to his wife.

"I don't think Jennifer Beaumount could fall in love with anything," I said, thinking it wasn't fair that she'd got her money after all.

"What goes around comes around," Blake said. "She'll get her comeuppance."

James ran his hand down Arnie's injured leg and said it shouldn't be too difficult to treat. "He'll always have to be on medication though," he added.

Hazel fed him some lettuce and Derek asked if he always stood as if he'd got two left feet.

"Just about," Hazel grinned. "He's pretty gormless really."

Cassandra said she thought he was lovely and carried on devouring the blackened sausages.

"I thought you were a vegetarian?" Katie caught her on the hop.

"Only at weekends," she blushed, and reached for another chicken leg.

"Wait till we tell Maxwell Curtis about this." Katie hadn't stopped talking about him since we called in at the House of Commons. He'd finally come round to the idea of supporting our campaign, especially now the PM had given it his blessing.

"That reminds me," Sarah said, opening a can of lager and passing it to Derek, "he's coming round here tomorrow night, wants to go over some papers with Trevor."

"What?" Trevor was momentarily caught with his mouth full and could only grin and wave his arm up and down. "But I can't," he finally spluttered, looking seriously rattled.

"Go on, you tell them." Hazel had suddenly become extremely coy.

"It's Hazel's birthday," Trevor fidgeted and then blurted out in a rush, "and we're going on a date."

James wolf-whistled and Ross patted him on the back. I dreamily thought how Trevor and

Arnie had a lot in common – they both had hidden depths.

Sarah said it was time we put Arnie to bed but Arnie had other things on his mind, namely Derek's lager.

"He thinks it's Guinness!" Hazel laughed hysterically. "He's so used to his daily pint."

Derek let out a howl as Arnie suddenly bulldozed after him, straight down the garden.

"Hadn't we better go and help him?" I tried to smother a giggle.

"We'd better send you-know-who to Alcoholics Anonymous," Sarah laughed.

As it was, Arnie finally settled for a cup of tea with lots of sugar.

The sun went down on one of the most momentous days at Hollywell Stables and Sarah finally managed to uncork the champagne bottle.

"Welcome to Hollywell!" We all toasted Arnie.

"We'd better read him the house rules," Ross grinned as Arnie butted him in the stomach. But somehow I didn't think Arnie was going to take the slightest bit of notice.

Samantha Alexander
Hollywell Stables 1

Flying Start £2.99

Hollywell Stables – sanctuary for horses and ponies. It was a dream come true for Mel, Ross and Katie . . .

A mysterious note led them to Queenie, neglected and desperately hungry, imprisoned in a scrapyard. Rescuing Colorado was much more complicated. The spirited Mustang terrified his wealthy owner: her solution was to have him destroyed.

But for every lucky horse at the sanctuary there are so many others in desperate need of rescue. And money is running out fast . . .

How can the sanctuary keep going?

Samantha Alexander
Hollywell Stables 2

The Gamble £2.99

Hollywell Stables – sanctuary for horses and ponies. It was a dream come true for Mel, Ross and Katie . . .

It was a gamble. How could it possibly work? Why should one of the world's most famous rock stars give a charity concert for Hollywell Stables? But Rocky is no ordinary star and when he discovers that the racing stables keeping his precious thoroughbred are cheating him, he leads the Hollywell team on a mission to uncover the truth . . .

Samantha Alexander
Hollywell Stables 3

Revenge £2.99

Hollywell Stables – sanctuary for horses and ponies. It was a dream come true for Mel, Ross and Katie . . .

Emotions run high at Hollywell stables when the local hunt comes crashing through the yard. The consequences are disastrous, and Charles Stonehouse is to blame.

Then one of the sanctuary's own ponies goes missing. Could the culprit be Bazz, who is back on the scene and out for revenge? The Hollywell team know they have to act fast: there's no time to lose . . .

Samantha Alexander
Hollywell Stables 4

Fame £2.99

Hollywell Stables – sanctuary for horses and ponies. It was a dream come true for Mel, Ross and Katie . . .

Rocky's new record, *Chase the Dream*, shoots straight into the Top Ten, and all the proceeds are going to Hollywell Stables. It brings overnight fame to the sanctuary and the family are asked to do television and radio interviews. On one show they get a call from a girl who has seen a miniature horse locked in a caravan, but she rings off before telling them where it was. The Hollywell team set off to unravel the mystery . . .

Samantha Alexander
Hollywell Stables 5

The Mission £2.99

Hollywell Stables – sanctuary for horses and ponies. It was a
dream come true for Mel, Ross and Katie . . .

A trip to a horse sale leads to a disturbing discovery – a mule
and a blind pony being loaded into a lorry in cramped conditions,
with no food or water. Mel, Ross and Katie hide in the lorry to
see what is to become of the ponies, but the plan backfires and
before they know it the lorry has set off for France . . .

It's the Hollywell team's most dangerous and exciting adventure
yet!